LA CAZADORA

THE HUNTRESS

Michael Aye

Book 10 of the Fighting Anthonys

Published by Boson Books
An imprint of Bitingduck Press
Formerly an imprint of C&M Online Media, Inc.
ISBN 978-1-68553-033-4
eISBN 978-1-68553-034-1

For information contact
Bitingduck Press, LLC
Altadena, CA
notifications@bitingduckpress.com
http://www.bitingduckpress.com

Author's note

This book is a work of fiction with a historical backdrop. I have taken liberties with historical figures, ships, and time frames to blend in with my story. Therefore, this book is not a reflection of actual historical events.

La Cazadora

the Huntress

The Fighting Anthonys
Book Ten

MICHAEL AYE

Books by Michael Aye

The Fighting Anthonys

The Reaper, Book One

HMS SeaWolf, Book Two

Barracuda, Book Three

SeaHorse, Book Four

Peregrine, Book Five

Trident, Book Six

Leopard, Book Seven

Ares, Book Eight

Andalucia, Book Nine

War of 1812 Trilogy

War of 1812: Remember the Raisin, Book 1

Battle at Horseshoe Bend, Book 2

Battle of New Orleans, Book 3

The Pyrate Trilogy

Pyrate, The Rise of Cooper Cain, Book One

Pyrate, Letter of Marque, Book Two

Pyrate, The Hunter, Book Three

Smugglers

The Smugglers of Deal

The Smuggler's Spy

Westerns

The Rise of the Gray Ghost

Fury in the South Pacific

Devil Boats, World War II

To:

All my Age of Sail readers who have waited for the final chapter in the Fighting Anthonys.

Troy, this one is for you!

Chris Bahnsen, you were a gentleman and a good friend. The world's a sadder place without your smiling face. I'll not forget you.

CHARACTERS IN *LA CAZADORA*, THE FIGHTING ANTHONY SERIES #10

His Majesty King George III
Lieutenant Colonel Robert Greville, - Equerry to King George III
George IV (Prinny), The Prince of Wales

Foreign Agents/Admiralty

Lord Randy Skalla –Foreign Service, Secret Division, Liaison to the Admiralty
First Lord Richard Howe, 5th Viscount Howe –First Lord of the Admiralty
Leo Gallagher – Foreign Service, Secret Division
Philip Stevens - First Secretary to Admiralty

British Navy Officers/Ships

HMS *Centaur* 74 - Flagship

Commodore Sir Gabe Anthony
Dagan – Gabe's uncle
Jake Hex – Gabe's cox'n
Josh Nesbit – Gabe's chef, gentleman's gentleman
Simon "hanged man" Davis – Gabe's secretary
David Davy – Flag captain
Fin Trehnock – Captain Davy's cox'n
Peter Dasher – First Lieutenant, later-Captain on HMS Nimble
Ted Danforth – Second Lieutenant
Robert Cope – Third Lieutenant
Ben Pittman- Master
Hunter Honeycutt – Physician, Surgeon
Onslow – Gunner
Oaks – Bosun
Joseph Morales – Carpenter
Phil LoGiudice – Marine
Noble "No" Pride Stanhope – Midshipman, later – Lieutenant

HMS *Nimble* (Sloop of War, 14 Guns)

Ronald Laqua – Captain, later-Captain of HMS *Active*

HMS *Active* 32, frigate

Ezekiel Wooten – Captain, lost at sea and Ronald Laqua assumes command

HMS *Thalis* 46, frigate

Chris Bahnsen – Captain

HMS *Venus* 32, frigate

Burnette Lee Honeycutt – Captain, father of Doctor Honeycutt

HMS *Warlock*

Troy Skidmore – Captain, previous captain on HMS Ferret 28, sunk
Peter Finch – Cox'n
Felix Myers – Servant
Paul Johns – First Lieutenant
Mr. Graves – Master
Lieutenant Hartley – Second Lieutenant
Noble Pride Stanhope – Third Lieutenant
Mr. Dartmouth – Marine Lieutenant
Christie – Gunner
Tabby – Bosun
Sidney Pilcher – Surgeon
Robert/Roberta Palmer – Woman masquerading as a man
Rawls – Midshipman
Padgett – Midshipman
Buntin – Midshipman

HMS *Thorn* (Sloop of War, 16 Guns)

Jeremy Calvert – Lieutenant, Captain

HMS *Storm* 36, frigate

Miles Bedford – Captain

Merchant Ships

WINDHAM, armed merchant ship

Sam Lee – Captain

SYBIL, merchant ship

Viggo Johanson –Captain

British Civilians

Lord William Stanhope – Earl of Gladstone
Maria Stanhope – Lord Stanhope's wife, and Gabe's mother
Sir Lawrence Cook – Doctor, Former foreign agent
Jimena Cook - Sir Lawrence's wife
Hugh English – Gabe's brother-in-law, and a Member of Parliament
Becky English – Hugh's wife and Gabe's sister
Gretchen English – Hugh and Becky's daughter, Noble's girlfriend
Kin Chantry – Lawyer and Gabe's agent, solicitor
Madison Honeycutt – Chantry's apprentice and Captain Honeycutt's daughter
Joe Moorer – Antigua Land owner and planter
Cecilia Moorer – Joe's wife
Faith Anthony – Gabe's wife
Ariel Davy – Captain Davy's wife
Robert Cornish – Doctor
Abida – Doctor Cornish's wife

Americans

Michael Manning – General
Betsy Manning – Dagan's love and wife
Andre Dupree – Maria and Dagan's uncle
Caleb McKean – Surgeon and Gabe's old friend
Kitty McKean – Andre's daughter, and Caleb's wife
Jubal Dupree – Andre's son
Hannah – Jubal's wife
Kawliga – Cherokee Indian, lives with Dupree

Frosty – Woodsman and guide
Gavin Lacy – Faith's uncle, her father's partner
Caroline – Gavin's wife

Antigua Dockyard

Rear Admiral Gardner
Greta Gardner – Gardner's wife

Island of Antigua

Vice Admiral Lord Gilbert Anthony – Governor of Antigua
Deborah Anthony – Lord Anthony's wife
Macayla Anthony – Lord Gilbert and Deborah's daughter
Bart – Lord Anthony's cox'n

The Bad Guys

Juan Alvarada – Captain on La Cazadora
Mateo Monterio – Captain of La Tigresa

San Juan

Pepe – Friendly coastal trader
Marianna – Puerto Rican girl kidnapped by Alvarada
Consuelo – Puerto Rican girl kidnapped by Alvarada

BAHAMA ISLANDS
HAVANA
CUBA
ISLA DE PINOS
SANTIAGO DE CUBA
TORTUGA
HAITI
SANTO DOMINGO
PORTO RICO
VIRGIN ISLES
ST CROIX
ST MARTIN
BARBUDA
ST CHRISTOPHER
NEVIS
ANTIGUA
MONTSERRAT
GUADELOUPE
MARIE GALANTE
THE SAINTS
DOMINICA
MARTINIQUE
ST LUCÍA
ST VINCENT
BARBADOS
GRENADA
TOBAGO
MARGARITA
JAMAICA
KINGSTON
CARIBBEAN SEA
CAPE GRACIAS A DIÓS
PROVIDENCE
HENRIETTA
MOSQUITO COAST
ARUBA
CURAÇAO
BONAIRE
LESSER ANTILLES
SANTA MARÍA

Part I

Thank God I Made It Home

The guns are all silent now
The ships been paid off
The peace has been signed
Now to pay the cost

Taken by the press gang
It seems forever in the past
Now I've got this empty sleeve
I feel the cannons blast

Now every way I turn
I can still feel that war
I'm not the only one
Cause there's hundreds more

Eight long years I fought that war
It cut me to the bone
I think of the mates I lost
Thank God I made it home

Michael Aye

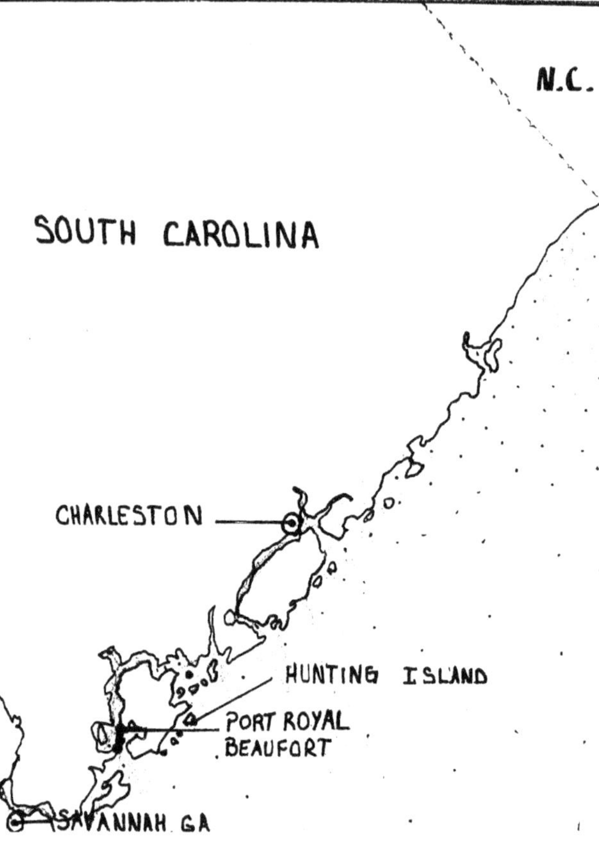
N.C.
SOUTH CAROLINA
CHARLESTON
HUNTING ISLAND
PORT ROYAL
BEAUFORT
SAVANNAH GA

PROLOGUE

IT WAS DAWN AND the men on Ferret, *much like those on the other ship patrolling with them, were at their battle stations. The captain of the* Ferret, *Troy Skidmore, waited anxiously for the sun to rise. He'd only been given command of the twenty-eight gun frigate a few months ago. It was just before the end of the hostilities with the Colonies…or as they were being called now, the Americans.*

The captain on the Spitfire *had held his commission a bit longer. Had it not been for the Peace Accord, Captain Baskins of the* Spitfire, *with twenty-eight guns, would probably have been given a larger frigate. For a man who had risen from a masters mate to the captain of a frigate, albeit a small one, it was a big jump. Baskins had caught the eye of Admiral Lord Gil Anthony. He'd passed his lieutenant exam with flying colors. He was soon under the command of Captain David Davy. When a prize had been taken, Baskins had been put on board. Since then his rise had been steady.*

Troy Skidmore, on the other hand, had been a lieutenant on a sloop, and then a third lieutenant on a thirty-eight gun frigate. When the captain, first and second lieutenants were killed, he took charge and sailed the crippled ship back to Bermuda. His reward had been command of a Bermuda sloop. He had given passage to Admiral Graves, who recommended him for a frigate. The luck had been with him and he had been given command of the Ferret, *frigate of twenty-eight guns. He had been assigned escort duty with a sixty-four gun ship and two other frigates.*

Once the supply ships made it to Bermuda, he was assigned as part of the Bermuda Squadron. With the peace now, they were to patrol in pairs and keep an eye out for pirates. The admiral in Bermuda had hotly stated the only difference between a privateer and a pirate was a damnable piece of paper. When the paper became null and void, the admiral asked his captains what did they think the rascals would do, take up yachting.

"The whoresons will do what they always do, prey on honest people," he shouted. He'd been right. Proof could be found hanging from the gallows along the waterfront of the Royal Navy Dockyard on Bermuda.

***

AMBER GLOWING CLOUDS HUNG over Havana as the dawn broke. Captain Skidmore, seeing nothing but a few fishing boats putting out to sea, felt both a sense of relief and disappointment. Without prizes, further upward mobility would be slow in coming.

The master made his way over to Skidmore. "I feel a squall is in the making." The captain nodded; the master was usually right.

Squawks off to larboard showed two gray gulls spreading their wings and swooping down, finding their breakfast as the morning sun rose. The sun above soon turned into a fiery red disc.

Skidmore's coat was removed and handed to Finch, Skidmore's handy cox'n. The white shirt beneath the coat was already soaked with sweat and was plastered to his body. Puddles of sweat ran down Skidmore's neck and down his spine. It was time to come about, but Baskins, being the senior, would say when. No sooner had Skidmore thought that, than Baskins made his move.

The squall showed itself as the hour passed. Key West

lay to larboard and Havana to starboard. The wind picked up and dark clouds blotted out most of the sun's rays and heat. When the rain came it was all at once, curtain after curtain. The ocean picked up, throwing wave after wave against the ship's hull and over the bow. Cascades of water came crashing on the deck, with some of it running down the channels and out the scuppers Skidmore felt his body shiver as the wind blew against his rain soaked clothes. As sudden as it had started, the rain stopped.

"Deck thar…a large ship coming up astern."

Damn fine report, Skidmore thought, thinking the man was still alert after riding out the storm in the tops. Skidmore stepped over to the rail and lifted his glass to get a look at the ship. He looked, brought his glass down and then looked again. She was a ship, a damn large ship, the type of which he'd never seen before.

"Another ship is coming up on Spitfire*'s stern," the lookout yelled.*

"To quarters," Skidmore yelled.

"All hands to quarters." The first lieutenant took up the call, hearing the urgency in his captain's voice. Hands scurried to their battle stations. "Come about, Captain?" the first lieutenant asked.

"No, we'll not give her a better target," Skidmore responded. "Two points to larboard," he ordered the helmsman. He'd not give the whoresons a broader target, but neither would he give them an easy one.

Skidmore felt the ship change as the wheel moved. He put the glass back up to his eye. What kind of ship is that, he asked himself again. Peering through the glass, he saw flames leap from the strange ship's bow guns before he heard the thunder. Balls hit the sea where Ferret had just been.

"Two more points to larboard," Skidmore called to the helmsman. The enemy ship fired and missed again. "Back to our original course," Skidmore yelled.

"Spitfire's been hit hard," the lookout called down.

Skidmore looked towards the Spitfire. That was a big Spanish frigate attacking Spitfire. But why...the peace treaty had been signed. The enemy ship fired again. One ball went through the sails and another hit the stern rail, sending pieces flying high in the sky. Were the aft guns not firing? They were the only ones that could bear.

Skidmore called to a midshipman, "Run aft and tell the gunners to fire."

The boy looked dumbfounded. "They have been, Captain." Skidmore nodded his head in response. He hadn't even noticed the guns firing.

The first lieutenant was back. "The Dons are closing fast, Captain."

Dons!!! He was right. "Come about, Mr. Spivey. We have to risk it, otherwise our rudder will be shot away and we'll not have a chance," Skidmore said.

BOOM...BOOM!!! Damme, that sounds like twenty-four pounders, Skidmore thought. We'll never match their metal as he thought, thinking about the size of the enemy guns.

Ferret gave a huge shudder as the balls slammed into the bulwarks and continued tearing a huge gouge in the deck planking and striking the main mast. Skidmore looked about at the devastation and the dead. The damnable enemy ship was now at pistol range. A load of ball and grape tore into his once beautiful ship. Skidmore's last thoughts were 'why...we are at peace.'

The next thing that Troy Skidmore knew was he was suspended in the air. Spitfire was sinking, and Ferret was ablaze. He thought he heard a voice...Finch? It was Peter Finch.

"Yes, cox'n," Troy willed himself to say. He felt himself crash into the water with a huge splash. He'd lost focus, and he could hear voices. Was someone tugging on him? God, he hurt. He felt himself drifting, like on a cloud. Then everything went blank.

CHAPTER ONE

GABE WATCHED FAITH AS she dressed. He felt his male humors rise and realized, even as long as they had been married and after having a child, she still stirred him. *If her maid had not been helping her*, Gabe thought, *I might see if I could stir her*. Time did not permit it though. They were due at Stanhope Hall in less than an hour. It was still hard for Gabe to grasp that his mother, a commoner no less, was now Lady Stanhope. Lord William Stanhope had fallen in love with her right off.

Gabe thought had his father lived, he would have been about the same age as Stanhope. It meant that his mother was younger by several years. She had lived well since Lord James Anthony had died. She had the house in Portsmouth. Gabe and Dagan had also provided her with added income and improvements to the property and even a couple of servants. As nice as the property was, it failed in splendor when compared to Lord Stanhope's London residence. Gabe just hoped that she'd be as happy there.

They had received an invitation earlier that day to dine at 8:00 p.m. with his mother and William...Lord Stanhope. It was hard to get used to calling him William.

"Are you ready, Gabe, the coach is waiting?" Faith asked.

"I'm sorry, Faith, my mind was adrift." He had not even noticed that Faith had finished dressing.

The gown Faith had on was sapphire blue. It didn't reveal as much of her breasts as a lot of the gowns that ladies wore did, but it gave more than a hint of what was hidden beneath it. *I'm glad that I'm the lucky man who gets to see those treasures*, Gabe thought. Remembering how young they were when they married, the beautiful girl had matured into a stunning woman. She's the spitting image of her mother, Nanny would say.

Gabe had planned to take Faith back to her family plantation when they reached America. What then, Gabe wondered. Dagan had no plans of going back to sea and Gabe didn't blame him. Dagan deserved to be happy with Betsy Manning. *Where is Dagan*, Gabe suddenly wondered. He'd last seen him at midday. Another thought came to Gabe, *neither had he seen Becky, Hugh, or Gretchen in hours*. It was unusual not to know what everyone was doing, especially since they were staying at Becky and Hugh's London house.

***

A LIVERIED DOORMAN WAS waiting when they reached Stanhope Hall.

"Evening, Sir Gabe, Lady Anthony."

"Evening, Rudolph," they replied.

"This way please," the doorman said.

They were led down a long hall to the saloon or great chamber. Gabe had only been to this part of the mansion once. It had been for the reception after his mother and Stanhope had married. The doorman announced them after the door was opened. Lord Stanhope, Gabe's mother, and a gentleman dressed in a formal uniform greeted them.

Lord Stanhope, after greeting Gabe and Faith, introduced the officer. "May I introduce you to Lieutenant Colonel Robert Greville. Colonel Greville is equerry to King George III."

Greville stepped forward and gave the most formal bow that Gabe had ever seen. His right leg dressed out in white silk stockings was extended so far out, Gabe was sure that the man would fall as he rocked back on his left leg and bowed.

When the bow was over, Greville repeated, "I'm the equerry to the Court of Saint James and His Majesty King George, the Third. I have come to arrange your presentation at Court in investiture of your baronetcy. The Crown would find it convenient should you be available to present yourself this Tuesday, January 22nd at 10:00 a.m. for the weekly levee." Gabe found himself nodding but totally lost. "Uniform and Court dress," Greville said.

Gabe found his voice and said, "Aye! Aye, sir."

Greville continued, "The formal notice and the requirements in dress has been placed in the care of Lord Stanhope. He has already given me a list of guests. Since you are the only one to be ennobled, the number of guests is not critical."

This seemed to end Greville's comments as he gave another legged bow and made his goodbyes, with Lord Stanhope personally showing him to the door.

Once they left, Gabe's mother came and hugged her son. "Your father would have been very proud of you, Gabriel."

Gabe felt close to losing his emotions. Thankfully, Lord Stanhope walked back in, and taking a glass from a servant's tray he raised it, "A toast to Sir Gabe Anthony, Baronet."

Dagan walked up and laid his hand on Gabe's shoulder. Looking at his uncle, Gabe said, "You deserve this more than I do."

"No, Gabe, I've advised you and you've made all the decisions. You have that from your father."

"I do wish that Gil could have been here," Gabe

said.

"Aye, Gabe, it would have been nice," Dagan replied.

One of Stanhope's people came in and announced that dinner was ready. Gabe was seated at Stanhope's right hand.

Gabe felt Faith touch his leg as they took their seats. He whispered to her. "You knew, didn't you?"

"Yes, but only as of today," Faith replied.

Looking around the table, Gabe saw several people that he hadn't seen in the saloon. Becky and Hugh were there. He remembered the first time meeting them was at his father's funeral. Gretchen had been a little girl back then. While Becky had hugged him, he couldn't have imagined how close he'd come to be with her and Hugh. Becky and Faith were like sisters. Gretchen...Gil had once called her a spoiled little snit. She was now a beautiful young lady, who seemed to be madly in love with No...Nobel Pride.

Nobel was the boy that Stanhope had refused to recognize. He had been raised a gutter snipe, and his mother had to become a little more than a whore to provide for the boy. The boy had royal blood and when it came time, he'd laid his life on the line against a group of rogues. Since Gabe and Francis Markham had shown him kindness, Nobel did his best to keep them from being ambushed and murdered. Stanhope recognized the boy now, thanks to Hugh, and tried to make amends for his former life. Mr. Nobel Pride Stanhope was now a midshipman and would soon sit for the lieutenant's exam. If they delayed the sailing dates again, he could maybe sit for the test before they left for the Colonies.

The others seated at the table included Dagan. He sat next to his sister, who was also Gabe's mother. Lord Skalla and his wife, Catherine, were seated next to Dagan. Sir Lawrence Cook and Jimena were there also, which was somewhat surprising to Gabe. There was talk that Sir Lawrence would end his duties and career making sure that all the prisoners of war were sent back to the United States. He was then going to look into moving to the Colonies. The thought being that Jimena would be closer to her home from there. Gabe thought as the Spanish had been an ally, Jimena would be more accepted there than in England.

***

FAITH AND GABE RODE to the palace with Lord Stanhope and Gabe's mother. As they were leaving, Hugh reminded him to wear his presentation sword. In all that finery, Hugh had teased, a hundred guinea presentation sword will look cheap, but it's the best we can do. Everyone laughed at Hugh's humor. Lord Stanhope's tailor had visited Gabe and had a team of his people working on Gabe's uniform. It was nothing short of perfect. When Gabe asked for the bill he was told not to concern himself with trivial matters, making him think that Stanhope had covered the cost of the uniform.

Gabe and Faith had lain awake talking after they'd made love the night that he'd been told of his baronetcy. "Who do you think put me up for this?" Gabe asked. "Was it Lord Skalla?" He'd wanted Gabe promoted to admiral but that was not to be. Had he talked to his friend, the Prince, to have the honor bestowed upon Gabe for his capture of the bullion galleons? It had to have helped fill the Crown's coffers, which years of war had dwindled. Did the idea come from the King? Had Stanhope, who was said to be friends with the King, recommend it."

Gabe had smirked at one point, and Faith said,

"What?"

"I was just thinking, you can damn well bet the Admiralty had nothing to do with it," Gabe replied.

Gabe's solicitor had said that Gabe's three-eighths of the value of the bullion alone made him the richest man in the Navy and near the top of England's richest men. He'd immediately been given over one-hundred thousand pounds toward his shares with the rest promised in quarterly increments,

"They want to earn a little interest on your money before they pay you," Hugh had japed.

As soon as they got to Saint James Palace, a liveried servant opened the door and spoke to Lord Stanhope. At the palace door another servant, whose outfit had so much gold lilt he looked like an army general, took their invitation. Another servant was quickly there and this time, he spoke to Stanhope and Gabe.

Gabe could see that both his mother and Faith were mesmerized by the palace, as they followed the servant. Grand staircases were done in marble, there were portraits of former kings and queens in larger-than-life frames, all in gold. The red and gold drapes ran over the top and down each side of the windows, and statues were everywhere. The high ceilings were all painted magnificently. The furnishings were huge and oversized.

Faith whispered, "I feel like a dwarf."

Their servant smiled, "It was quite overwhelming for me as well, but I've grown used to it now."

Gabe was about give out by the time they reached the last hall that the servant took them too.

"This is where the levee will be held," the servant said, and then he spoke to another servant.

People were milling about, talking to first one and then another. Men, who were obviously rich or titled or both, stood about. Some of the men looked young but most of the men were older. There were surprisingly few ladies. The ones that were there were with mostly older men. Gabe caught one elegantly gowned lady actually looking him up and down. Her gown was so low that if she were to bend over her nipples would be exposed. Gabe felt a set of fingernails bite into his arm.

"Tramps are tramps. Money or not," Faith hissed.

"What's that, my dear," the woman asked.

Gabe thought, *shat we're about to be escorted from the palace.*

"I said that there are so many here, I'm afraid we might get trampled," Faith replied.

The woman smiled and asked, "It's your first time here?"

"Yes," Faith admitted.

"Hold tight to your man, dear, or some frustrated woman will lead him astray," the woman said.

Faith smiled, "I'm not frustrated and he's well taken care of but if a woman can take him away from me, I don't know him as well as I think I do."

"Well said, dear. I like you and I can see that he has eyes only for you. I'm Lady Serville. Madalyn to my friends. I think that we could be friends," she said. "Where can I send an invitation for us to have lunch?"

Faith was now relaxed and smiling, "Either at Lord Stanhope's, or the residence of Hugh and Becky English."

Madalyn put her hand to her mouth, "Your husband is Becky's brother."

"Yes," Faith replied. A man was making an announcement, at that time, so Madalyn mouthed goodbye.

"If you'll come with me," the man was saying to Gabe.

Gabe smiled and squeezed Faith's hand. They

walked towards the front of the crowd, and Gabe spied Dagan. He'd never seen his uncle so attired. *Stanhope again*, Gabe thought.

"My lords and ladies, gentlemen, and gentle women," the man was saying. "The King."

Amidst the routine honors, the king made his way forward. Gabe lowered his head, having been instructed by Lord Stanhope's man. Faith did as well, but she peeked at all the others. She thought that King George needed to cut back on his eating as he was somewhat portly. The queen was next, and then George IV, who some called Prinny.

Faith had met the prince a few times. *Did he recognize me?* His hand brushed her sleeve as he walked by. He must have recognized her or perhaps sees her as another challenge to get in his bed chamber. Had Gabe noticed the prince's touch? *Hmmm*, she wondered. *No man has ever touched me before, not even on the arm...well, outside of family,* she thought.

As quick as the man finished announcing the queen, the prince was announced. When the prince was seated, a man banged on the floor.

"The ceremonial mace," Stanhope whispered at the thud...thud...thud.

A man then called, "Commodore Sir Gabriel Anthony KB."

Gabe, following Stanhope's man's instructions, made his way forward and made his, he hoped, satisfactory bow.

"Sir Gabe," the king said, leaving off Gabe's navy rank. *Is his mental illness affecting him,* Gabe wondered? "In grateful recognition," the king paused, and seemed to peer at a document a courtier, next to him, was holding. The king then pushed the document away with a little laugh. He started again and said, "In recognition of your unimaginable success and service to this country and me personally, and in honor of your service as a commissioned sea officer of some renown in our Royal Navy. I do now name thee Baronet of Great Britain."

"Thank you very much, your Majesty," Gabe spoke softly. "I am honored to meet you and be rewarded in such a fashion."

"Think nothing of it," the king replied. "William has told me of your service. No one is more deserving. Now be gone before this fellow starts growling." Saying this, the king looked up at the courtier, who remained stoic.

Trying not to smile, Gabe saw the king looked at him once more. *Damme, I believe he just winked,* Gabe thought as he made his way back. They were soon led to another Great Hall where a reception was being held.

Lord Stanhope was late arriving, but when he did he was accompanied by the prince. Faith felt her heart jump. *The damn man better not touch me*, she thought. The prince greeted Gabe and her, and then made his departure.

CHAPTER TWO

IT WAS FEBRUARY, 1784. A coach pulled up to the front of the inn. The driver was hunched over trying to keep the rain from running down inside his coachman's coat, or Garrick. Three men got out of the coach, Commodore Sir Gabe Anthony BT KB., his cox'n, Jake Hex, and Mr. Midshipman Noble "No" Pride Stanhope.

The drizzle was picking up and making for a miserable night for any traveler or those standing watch on board the many ships in Portsmouth Harbor. Several of his Majesty's captains were inside waiting to meet their new commander.

The wind was freshening from out of the south, and hopefully the boat crews, who had brought their captains ashore, were tucked away somewhere dry. The cox'n or midshipman was hopefully keeping an eye out to make sure no one got drunk. Overhead the gray clouds had momentarily blocked out most of the moon.

"It will get worse before it gets better," Jake Hex said. There weren't many cox'ns who would have spoken as he had, but the relationship between Sir Gabe and Hex went much further than the usual captain-cox'n relationship. Jake had saved a younger Gabe from being strangled to death by a prisoner in a cell when Gabe had made the mistake of turning his back on the man. Hex had turned down the offer of sitting for the lieutenant's exam and becoming an officer. He felt that he'd live a much better life attaching himself to the boy captain whom he was sure would be an admiral one day. Gabe's father and brother had each made flag, so Hex was sure that Gabe would also, especially now that he had very influential backers.

Gabe had, after all, just been made a baronet and had also filled the English treasure with thousands of pounds of Spanish silver and gold. He was now rich as a Moorish sultan or a British nabob.

Glancing out to sea before entering the George Inn, Gabe could see that the sea was getting lively. He couldn't see the *Solent* but if its sheltered waters were becoming as alive as those closer in shore, it would indeed be a bad night. Jake had been right in his comment but he usually was.

No, officially known as Mr. Stanhope pushed open the door of the inn. The heat inside the inn rushed to meet them. A servant rushed forward and took Gabe's cloak, but Hex reached for Gabe's hat since it was new. Hex would not trust it to some inn servant.

Gabe, hearing the unmistakable voice of his flag captain, David Davy, turned to the room's door. The laughter following Captain Davy's comments ceased when No opened the door. Seeing their commodore, the officers all rose and a silence fell over the group. Gabe motioned with his hands for them to return to their seats.

Davy stepped forward as the men went back to their seats. "If I may, Sir Gabe. A toast to Sir Gabe on his Baronetcy."

The men all stood and raised their glasses, "To Sir Gabe."

When they had all sat back down, Gabe smiled. "It seems that you all know who I am. However, I'd like to get to know each of you. I recognize Captain Lee, so we'll start with you and then go around the room."

Lee stood up and said, "Sam Lee of the merchant ship, *Windham*. It's good to see you again, Sir Gabe. I hope this trip will be as successful as our last one."

Sam is letting everyone know that we have a history together, Gabe thought. *Smart man*.

"Viggo Johnson, captain of the merchant ship, *Sybil*." Gabe nodded.

"Chris Bahnsen, captain, HMS *Thalis* 36, sir."

Gabe quickly asked, "Do you have a relative who is going with us?"

Captain Bahnsen smiled, "My father is General John Bahnsen, sir. He is the army general assigned to making sure all of our guests have been placed on board a vessel and sent home." Bahnsen got a laugh at those comments.

"We'll try to make his job easy," Gabe responded. This got another laugh.

The next captain stood, "Zeke Wooten, captain, HMS *Active* 32, sir."

"It's a fine ship that you've been given," Gabe said.

"That's what I understand, sir," Wooten replied. His words seemed to be less than energetic.

"What was your last command, Captain?" Gabe asked.

"The frigate, *Reliant*, sir, thirty-six guns," Wooten responded.

Hmm, he likely sees this as a step backwards, Gabe thought, *but with all the ships being decommissioned, he was lucky to get a fine ship like Active*. "Glad to have you, sir," Gabe offered.

The next captain stood, "Lee Honeycutt, captain, HMS *Venus* 32, sir."

"You were with Admiral Knight's squadron a few years ago, were you not, Captain?"

"Aye, sir. It's good of you to remember. It was the old *Belle Poule*, sir. She'd long been past her prime. I feel lucky to have been given the *Venus*."

Gabe was about to speak when Honeycutt added, "*Venus* is a crack frigate, Commodore. She'll not let you down."

A man with pride in his ship, Gabe thought. *I wish that Wooten was as enthused*. 'Well said, Captain," Gabe responded. He let his eyes go back over the room. He'd expected to see Laqua there. Had he misheard that the *Nimble* would be part of the group?

"Gentlemen, my orders are few. Mainly, every man is to do his duty. A messenger will bring around a set of orders for you, probably in the next twenty-four hours." When he looked around the room, he saw that Wooten was staring at something or somebody. Gabe followed Wooten's gaze and saw that it was on Hex. *He doesn't like Hex being with a body of officers*, Gabe thought.

"Captain Davy and I have known each other for years," Gabe said. "We were midshipmen together at one time. I have the utmost confidence in him as flag captain. Jake, step forward. This man should be wearing the commodore's uniform, not I," Gabe said. "He has been at my side through more battles than some of you can imagine. He often carries out errands for me...verbally at times. If he boards your ship, you can bet that I sent him and I expect him to be treated with respect and dignity." A chair scraped the floor and Gabe wasn't sure but it seemed to come from Wooten's area. "Let me just make this plain, gentlemen. If I send Hex to your ship, it's to convenience both you and I. But, if he's not treated as I expect him to be, you can bet the next time I need you, it will be at my convenience on board the flagship."

Bahnsen, who was the senior captain present, outside of Davy spoke, "Understood, Sir Gabe." He then turned to Hex and said, "You are most welcome aboard the frigate, *Thalis*, or I'll know why." Several here...here's went up, but Wooten was not one of them.

They went over a few more details and then Gabe made ready to go. Ariel was at Gabe's mother's house, where Gabe was now staying, until it was time to sail. He leaned over and whispered to Davy, "The women plan dinner for 8:00."

Davy smiled and then looked at his timepiece, "I'll be on time."

***

DAGAN ARRIVED AT THE house in Portsmouth just as the rains picked up. A quick dash inside kept him from getting soaked to the skin. He'd just settled down with a glass of wine when Faith came down. Dagan looked at her and said, "Maria and Stanhope will be here tomorrow."

"I thought that they would be," Faith replied.

"I'd be surprised if they don't have a guest," Dagan added.

Faith looked at this man that she'd come to love like a father. She said, as they made eye contact, "Gretchen."

Dagan smiled and nodded, "Aye, and they say that *I* have a gift."

Faith smiled and replied, "Yours is real, but I know love when I see it, and Gretchen is madly in love with No. So much so that, she'd run off with him if she had to."

Dagan didn't dispute Faith. She would be the one to know. "I wouldn't doubt," Dagan said, "if she were to drop some not so subtle hints that she'd like to go to America and on to Antigua with you. She's finished all her studies. So there's nothing to keep her in England except Becky and Hugh. And there's one big reason to see America and Antigua."

Faith smiled again and responded, "No."

"Aye, that's the long and short of it as my Betsy would say." Dagan replied.

"I'll talk to Gabe," Faith said. "Hopefully, Hugh and Becky understand that we can't chaperone them every minute of the day." Dagan nodded and Faith took a deep breath and gave a sigh. "To think that at their age they'll not explore each other's...bodies."

"Well, no more than any others at that age," Dagan said.

Faith looked at him and said, "You could maybe give No a talk."

Dagan smiled again, "No became a man while we were gone. Fairly raped as it was...at first anyway. We know that he's tasted passion's fruit, but he said that he'd never violate Gretch, as he calls her." A noise at the front door ended the conversation.

"Uncle, you're back," Gabe said, as he kissed Faith.

A servant came and took his boat cloak and hat, and then took Hex's, as Gabe continued, No will come with David."

Faith nodded and replied, "Ariel is freshening up."

"Was your trip successful?" Gabe asked Dagan.

"Aye, I saw Kin Chantrys. He's taken a female assistant who is going to read law with him. What makes this so interesting is that this young lady is the daughter of one of your captains."

"What's her name?" Gabe asked.

"Honeycutt, Madison Honeycutt," Dagan answered.

"Her father is Lee Honeycutt, captain of the *Venus*. He seems like a decent man, glad to have a ship, unlike some," Gabe said. Dagan raised his eyebrow, and Gabe replied, "Captain Wooten. He was given command of the frigate, *Active*. I get the feeling that he was expecting something bigger. I get the impression that he might also have a short temper, from his manner with Hex. Even a flogging tarter. If we had more time, I would look into his background a bit. Maybe he has a backer, but putting him in a smaller frigate is a way to get his attention."

"You usually don't change those types of people," Dagan answered. Reaching in his pocket, he pulled out a receipt from Coutt's bank for a deposit. "You know that you could quit the sea," he said.

Faith spoke up then, "What would he do?"

Gabe gave her a gentle pop on the butt, "Keep you barefoot and pregnant."

"Gabe!" Faith hissed but smiled. She never did get to go out to dine with her new friend from the palace. If she had, maybe she'd have learned how to handle her man. She turned away and then thought of something. "There's a letter for you from Doctor Cornish."

Gabe rushed to it eagerly but he frowned as he read the letter. "We'll need a new doctor. Now that he's married, Cornish wants to spend some time with his wife. He is thinking of making his home in America, as are other people." There was some more noise heard from the front of the house. "That will be David and No."

"I'll go tell Ariel," Faith volunteered.

Later that night at dinner, Gabe broke the news that Cornish had turned down the role as ship's surgeon.

"What do you think of taking a chance on a new physician?" David asked.

A doctor like Cornish who wasn't just a surgeon, but Gabe asked anyway, "Do you have one in mind?"

"Captain Honeycutt gave me a letter from his son earlier in the week. I told him that you were in communication with our old physician, but I would contact him as soon as I heard from you."

"*Centaur* is your ship, Captain. Since our friend has chosen to become a land lubber, I leave it to you to select our new physician," Gabe replied.

"Thank you, sir," David said. "It's like you said, though, friends first."

After supper, Faith told Gabe about Gretchen. He looked at her and said, "In truth, Faith, it's more up to you. She could be a burden, but she could, just as well, be a big help and a friend. I don't foresee any real separations for a while but we could go to war tomorrow."

"I know," Faith responded and kissed Gabe a long passionate kiss.

When they broke apart, Gabe smiled, "I've got you barefoot, now let's see if I can get you naked."

CHAPTER THREE

HMS *NIMBLE* ARRIVED THE next day. She was much different than what Gabe had been expecting. She was not a brig as he'd been told but a ship rigged, flush deck sloop of war. She was pierced for fourteen guns but looking through his glass, Gabe could also see two carronades mounted on the forecastle. A boat was over the side of *Nimble* and her captain, Lieutenant Ron Laqua, was on his way to the flagship almost as soon as the signal for 'captain to repair on board' was raised. Gabe had to restrain himself from going topside to welcome his friend. It was Captain Davy's job now.

The marine soon announced, "Flag captain, sir." Davy entered with Laqua in tow, and Gabe rose up to meet his friend.

"Sorry I'm late joining, Sir Gabe. The minute I joined the ship, I was sent on escort duty," Laqua explained.

Gabe waved away Laqua's apology. "I'm surprised at your ship, Ron. I was expecting a brig."

"Aye, Sir Gabe, so was I. My orders stated HMS *Nimble*, brig of fourteen guns. The captain that I relieved said he'd informed the Admiralty when he commissioned her that she was not a brig nor a brig sloop, but a sloop-of-war. He received a letter back telling him any ship below twenty guns was termed a sloop-of-war and that encompassed all unrated combat vessels, including gun brigs, cutters, bomb vessels, and fireships. Deciding that he'd done his duty he attached the Admiralty's letter with a fair copy of his letter complete with date and signature. He left it for me to include in my papers."

"Smart man," Gabe said, and then added, "you know our Lords at the Admiralty don't make mistakes. What do you need to make your ship ready for sea?"

"Water and provisions," Laqua said. "My gunner has found a barrel of gunpowder that has loose staves and leaks powder if it's moved."

"We'll notify the port admiral. Is there anything else?" Gabe asked.

Laqua dropped his eyes. "I was hoping for a couple of days off, sir, to see my mother and sister. I haven't had a chance to see them since we were first sent to Antigua."

Gabe realized that it had been several years. "Do you trust your first lieutenant?" he asked.

"Aye, sir. I think that he was a bit resentful when *Nimble* came to me rather than him. He has been on her since she was first commissioned. Unfortunately, her service for such a fine ship has been unremarkable. She's basically been a dispatch vessel. According to her logs, she's never fired a shot at the enemy. I maybe shouldn't have said it, but I told him not to expect a Sunday cruise being under your command, sir." Davy laughed, as did Dagan and Hex, who walked in, in time to hear the comments.

"When you get back, we'll have a final meeting with all the captains so you'll get a chance to meet everyone," Gabe replied.

"Aye, aye, sir. As I was being rowed past *Active* we could hear the cat being laid on some poor soul," Laqua volunteered.

Gabe stiffened and said, "Did you know about this,

Captain Davy?"

"No sir, I did not," Davy replied.

"See if you can find out what's the reason for this."

"Aye," Davy responded.

Gabe turned back to Laqua, "I intend to sail on Monday. When you return to your ship by Sunday morning, I will have your needs completed."

"Thank you, Sir Gabe."

"Ron, if asked where you're going, it might be better if you were running an errand for me," Gabe said.

"Aye, sir, and what errand might that be?"

Gabe smiled and responded, "To deliver my well wishes to your family. But it's no one's business what your errand is. That it's for me is enough."

"Thank you again, Sir Gabe."

"Be gone with you, sir."

Once Laqua was gone, Gabe spoke to Davy, "When Laqua is ashore, it wouldn't hurt for you to go on board *Nimble* and let the first lieutenant know that while his captain is performing a service for me, he can call on you for anything."

"Aye."

"David!"

"Yes, sir."

"Find out about the flogging," Gabe said.

"Aye sir," Davy replied.

"I don't like it one bit. In fact, I'll not tolerate it," Gabe said.

"Aye, sir, I'll get to the bottom of it," Davy responded.

***

GABE WAS GETTING READY to go ashore when Dagan walked in. Since the marine sentries had been instructed that Dagan had an open door policy, Gabe didn't realize his uncle had entered until a shadow fell over the desk, where he was signing orders to be sent out to the ships in the squadron. Looking up, he saw Dagan's face, and it looked troubled.

"Yes!" Gabe said.

"I wish that you had time to have Wooten replaced. I happened by a shore party and heard some comments that I didn't like. Mind you, I think I was meant to hear them; not unlike a cry for help," Dagan said.

Gabe nodded, "And they were saying?"

"Men who have never had a mark against them have been flogged for trivial infractions. One man was flogged for laughing at a joke while they were holystoning the deck. Wooten took it as a remark that was made against him. The first lieutenant came to the sailor's defense but Wooten rebuked him in front of the entire crew. He blames the men under him in his last command for his not getting a 'prime or premier' command. He told the first lieutenant that the culls of the waterfront cost him once and they'd never do it again. He also told the first lieutenant in front of the crew that if the officers didn't support him, as was his right, he'd make damn sure they never sailed again. Ledford, the second lieutenant, spoke out where he could be heard, saying that he could give a good dammit all. His father was Lord Danforth and he'd gotten him his billet aboard *Active* as she was a proper ship with a historic reputation. One letter to his father and then Wooten could be damned. Wooten then made an announcement that all mail going on shore would be read by him."

"Damn the man, Dagan. Who does this idiot take me for, to think that I'll allow him to get by with this? Josh," Gabe called.

"Aye, sir."

"My compliments to Captain Davy and ask him to see me at his convenience."

"Yes, sir," Josh replied. Captain Davy was only minutes in reporting.

Gabe asked, "Did you speak to Wooten about flogging?"

"Yes, sir. He basically told me that unless he was being brought before a court martial, discipline on board his ship was his damn business."

"Signal for him to 'repair on board'," Gabe requested. "You then go talk to his officers."

"Aye, Sir Gabe," Davy answered.

"You bring me back the truth," Gabe said.

"Aye," Davy replied.

Captain Wooten was slow in reporting, giving the excuse that he was down in the hold when word came to him.

Gabe politely explained that he was concerned about the number of floggings on board *Active*. "I'm very surprised," he said.

Active had been under his command for most of the previous year with the same crew, and there had been no floggings during that time.

Wooten drew himself up and spoke, "I find that Captain Davy was much too lax. He allowed the crew liberties far beyond anything I've ever encompassed. I'm afraid his laxity has even corrupted the officers, so much so that they make excuses for the men when I know for certain they have been insolent and insubordinate."

Gabe stood up, "Captain Wooten, you are making very disparaging remarks against your flag captain. Were he here, I'm sure that he'd demand satisfaction." Wooten paled at Gabe's words "Remember Captain, you can be held accountable for such remarks."

"I thought that we spoke in confidence," Wooten muttered.

"Another thing, Captain, if you were to check *Ac-*

tive's record it is beyond reproach. Have you been in combat, Captain, where you were outnumbered two to one? And the only chance you have of winning the day is the fierce determination of the crew to fight to the last."

"I've not been in combat," Wooten said.

"What? You've not been in battle!"

"No, sir."

"I wish to God that you had, sir," Gabe exclaimed. "You'd then see your life and your ship dependent on the men. Men that you've flogged and belittled. Well, let me tell you, Captain, that ship and those men have been in combat time and again, and they've not once lost the battle. You better think of that the next time you order a flogging or belittle an officer in front of the crew. One more thing, Captain, your flag captain and I were midshipmen together, and as a close friend, I take it personally when you make negative comments about him."

"I should have known," Wooten muttered.

"What!! What did you say, Captain?" Gabe furiously asked.

"It was nothing...it was nothing, sir," Wooten replied.

Gabe hissed, "This is our only meeting, Captain. The next time that I call you on board, it will be to place you under arrest."

"Is that all, Commodore?"

"It's not by a damn sight. Had I had more time, I'd have you replaced. Keep that in mind." Gabe responded.

"Yes, sir."

"You are dismissed."

"Yes, sir."

A thought came to Gabe. "Captain Wooten!"

"Yes, sir."

"There is no need to screen a person's mail, as we are not at war. In fact, I'm giving you an order not to. Do you understand?"

"Yes, sir."

"I will send you that order in writing."

"Yes, sir."

"Good day, Captain, and it would be in your best interest to take heed of my words," Gabe said.

"Yes, sir."

When Wooten left, Dagan came from behind the screen to Gabe's sleeping area. "Bad business, that one."

"I agree," Gabe responded.

CHAPTER FOUR

IT WAS TIME TO sail, at last. General Bahnsen had met with Gabe the evening before and related that the last of the Americans were safely on board their ship. It had come as no surprise that Doctor Cornish and Doctor Lawrence Cook had become friends. The friendship had started when Cook had been assigned to the Caribbean a few years earlier. Both doctors, with foreign wives, had now decided to go into a medical practice together. Hopefully, around Norfolk or maybe nearer to Dagan's uncle's place near Petersburg. It was also where Gabe's old comrade, Caleb, had settled after marrying. Caleb was also a doctor. It was in Gabe's mind to visit his relatives if at all possible.

Gabe walked on deck feeling a bit of excitement, as he always did, when his ship weighed anchor and set sail...only now it wasn't his ship. She was his flagship, but *Centaur* was Captain Davy's ship. No was speaking with Davy. He must have noticed Gabe and told his captain.

Davy walked over to his commodore, "Signal from the admiral, sir. 'God's speed and fair winds'." Almost on cue, when Davy mentioned signals, a flapping noise was heard aloft. It was Gabe's broad pendant. "A beautiful sight, if you ask me, Commodore," Davy said.

"Thank you, David," Gabe replied.

"The anchor's hove short, sir." This was from the First Lieutenant Peter Dasher. *A funny name*, Gabe thought. Davy really liked the man, though. They had been together for some time, off and on.

A voice caused Gabe to turn his head. Faith had been giving the carpenter, Joseph Morales, a list of things required for their quarters. One, a small bed for James that wouldn't see him slung arse over tea kettle if the sea got up.

Morales raised his eyes a bit at Faith's description. "Yes, my lady," he said.

She then discussed the need for a screen partition to be put up for Nanny and one for Gretchen. *Yes, dammit*, Gabe thought, *Gretchen*. Once he thought about it, he realized his ability to make love to Faith while at sea was not going to happen...*damn the luck*.

Morales had a couple of his mates with him. One of them was carrying a rolled up canvas and wood, while the other mate had an armload of tools. Faith had never asked for any refitting like this before. Of course, she had only sailed in frigates.

Gabe heard a thud and "oof". He looked around and saw that it was the new doctor, Hunter Honeycutt, who had fallen. He'd been speaking to Faith about James. The lad had developed a sniffle and a cough. Hearing Gabe's little boy cough, the doctor volunteered to check him out. He'd been in Gabe's cabin for some time now, and Gabe wasn't sure if he'd not been checking out Gretchen, as well. *I better have Hex or Dagan drop a hint*, Gabe thought as he gave the doctor a hand up.

"One must remember to lift his feet a bit higher," Dagan was saying, but he didn't extend a hand to help. When Gabe looked at his uncle, Dagan just smiled.

"Thank you, Sir Gabe. Captain Davy has promised it will all come to me," the doctor said.

"And so it shall...so it shall," Gabe replied, turning

his attention back to the men going about their duties of getting the ship underway.

Davy had just spoken to Lieutenant Dasher, "Get the ship underway, if you please, Mr. Dasher. Lay a course to weather the headland."

"Aye, Captain."

Oaks, the bosun, without waiting to be ordered by the first lieutenant, took up the cry, "Hands aloft! Loose topsails."

Bare feet thudded across the deck planks. The doctor gave a little gasp as the riggings and shrouds were suddenly alive with men swarming up them. Topmen ran aloft like sure-footed monkeys. A man that was too slow about his duties was cursed for a laggard and struck by a rope end...*whap*. The man found that he could move a bit faster with that bit of encouragement. Honeycutt looked on.

"It was nothing doctor, sometimes a man will get lax if allowed," Dagan explained.

"Break out the anchor," Dasher shouted.

Oaks had moved into position. "Heave," he shouted to the men. "Put yer backs into it. Smith, I sees why yer old lady left ye. You're a whimpering, old woman." Oaks cane came down...*whack*. "You'll be a man when we comes back, Smith. Heave now." The capstan cranked and a clank, clank, clank was heard. "None of you are worth a pair of worn out whore's drawers. Heave now." There were other commands that were shouted out, "Loose headsails."

The doctor leaned his head back straining his neck watching from above. The canvas came down from above, flapping in the wind and then banged taut, while men were out some distance on the swaying yards grappling with the sail.

"A hand for the ship and a hand for yourself," Dagan volunteered, remembering his days as a topman.

From forward, Lieutenant Cope shouted, "Anchor's aweigh, sir."

Centaur paid off into the wind, almost like Gabe's old frigate, *Ares*. The deck heeled sharply, so Gabe braced himself. Thankfully, Dagan gave a hand to the doctor as a gust of wind filled the sails.

"Man the braces," Dasher shouted out.

"Look alive," a burly petty officer bellowed out.

As the men at the braces strained and heaved until the yards began to come around, Honeycutt whistled. *I see that there'll be a few ruptures before the cruise is over,* he thought.

Dagan leaned close to the doctor, "Sailors are a superstitious lot. One is against whistling. It is said that if you whistle, you'll whistle up a storm. Luckily, I don't think anyone heard you."

Honeycutt swallowed, "I'm not sure that I'm cut out for the sea."

"Give it time," Dagan said, with a smile. The billowing canvas thundered out hard making the doctor jump. "It's nothing but the wind filling out the sails," Dagan said. "See how the ship is moving fast."

From the bow, someone called, "Anchor is catted and made fast."

Dagan explained that the term catted home and made fast meant the anchor had been placed in the cathead, which was a heavy piece of curved timber sticking out from bow for the specific purpose of holding anchors. It was then made fast by ropes so that it wouldn't swing loose in a heavy sea.

Gabe spoke then, "Feel free to ask any of the senior hands, including Dagan or Hex, if you have a question. It's good to see you on deck taking an interest in the handling of the ship. By knowing the way of things, you'll understand the hardships that the men face better." Honeycutt nodded his head in response.

Taking his glass, Gabe watched as each ship fell in line behind the flagship…all but one.

"Damme," Captain Davy snarled. "That man handles *Active* like she was some damn fishmonger's scow."

Gabe gritted his teeth. A fine ship degraded by a worthless captain. Maybe he should relieve the man now. He could signal *Nimble* and once she closed, he could board her and then board *Active*, putting his first lieutenant in charge temporarily. It began to drizzle then, so Gabe said, "Keep an eye on *Active*, Captain."

"Aye," Davy acknowledged.

Once Gabe was in his cabin, out of the weather, he was astonished at the work that had been done by Morales and his mates. The clerk's cabin had been given to Gretchen. Next to it a screen, much like the one in the wardroom, had been built for Nanny. A small cot was also slung there for James. His clerk and Josh were to share the steward's room on the orlop deck. He felt bad for his men being displaced, but he told Josh if there was room in the pantry, to sling a hammock there if he wished.

When everyone was out of hearing, Gabe spoke to Faith. "I see you managed to keep us some private space."

Faith smiled and said, "I've come to enjoy my husband at my side. Besides, we have a private toilet."

"Head," Gabe corrected.

"Aye, mate," Faith quipped, "or is it 'seat of ease?'"

Gabe smiled, "That's at the bow."

"Where is Lum?" Faith asked.

"I have him with Morales' mates. They all have something in common," Gabe replied.

Faith nodded and then gave a sigh, "They wouldn't want to hear me say it, Gabe, but Nanny and Lum are both starting to show some age."

"I've noticed," he agreed. "Hopefully, life will be easier for them."

Faith nodded, "I told Nanny that we'd get someone to help her if she wanted me to." She smiled, "Nanny said 'Hush yo mouth, girl, 'fore I tan yo backside.'" Gabe had to smile.

"Dah, Dah!" Little James came running to him. Gabe leaned over and picked up his son.

"He's already been over most of the ship," Hex said. Uncle Jake had been doing his part to keep the little man entertained.

"Thank you, Jake," Faith said.

She often felt so sorry for Jake Hex. The only woman he had ever really loved turned out to be a spy for the enemy. *Would he ever find the right woman*? She didn't know. Enough of them fairly threw themselves at him. He didn't go lacking for willing maidens. But would he find love again? She wasn't sure.

If something happened to Gabe would she love again? She didn't think so. Not unlike Jake and his woman, Gabe had been the enemy. There he was, a wounded British naval officer, lying in the mud outside Beaufort, South Carolina when she found him. She was instantly in love. She'd taken him back to their plantation. When her uncle found him, he'd been put in chains. When Dagan came to his rescue, he told her that he'd be back. She'd waited and when he came, she left with him. She was glad the damnable war was over. She wanted to live as normal a life as a woman could being married to a sea officer.

Ariel was feeling a lot of the same feelings, Faith had felt. Were the two of them not close and able to support each other, Faith didn't know what she would have done. At least their husbands were frequently together. Ariel was pregnant now. The doctor had been there to check on Ariel. Everyone thought that he was there to see James, and he did, but it was Ariel who he really came for. Now that she was sure of her pregnancy, she'd inform Davy. *There was so much going on*, Faith thought, *and them at sea*.

CHAPTER FIVE

IT SEEMED THAT THE dark clouds with intermittent rain intended to follow them all the way to America. On board the two leased ships, *Windham* and *Sybil*, conditions had to be worse. The seas tended to be rougher in the morning and at dinner...mealtimes. How *Centaur* had managed to remain a private ship, if you could call it that, with Major LoGuidice's wife Holly, Captain Davy's wife, Ariel, and the Anthony group was amazing.

No had been invited to dine on two occasions. This had been Faith's doing. It was to Noble 'No' Pride Stanhope's credit that he refrained from any interaction with Gretchen when on duty, other than a smile and a pleasant word in passing. Once, in the great cabin, Gabe had explained that No had to carry out his duties regardless of who was on board the ship. Were he to shirk his duties and get reported, he'd be disciplined, and that would not be something pleasant for either of them. Both of them understood that.

Gretchen, then, as mature as she could be, said the dumbest thing, "I wish that he'd hurry up and make captain." When Gabe laughed, Gretchen got defensive. "Mother said that you were a boy captain."

Gabe controlled his humor. "Yes, but I'd been a midshipman for years before I was eligible to take the lieutenant examination. We were then at war and I was given a prize ship to command. I'd already been wounded." Gabe said this, touching his scalp where the white streak was. If the ball that did this had been just a touch closer, I'd have been killed. A lot of good men, many friends of mine, died, so we have to be careful of what we wish for…we might get it."

When he finished, Gretchen's eyes were watery. She leaned in and hugged him, "I'm sorry, Uncle Gabe. I don't mean to sound so selfish."

"I know you don't, honey. You can ask Faith and Ariel, it takes a special kind of woman to love a sea officer. Not every marriage can stand it, the loneliness and sacrifice. You know that he will become the Earl when Lord Stanhope dies."

"That's already been taken care of," Gretchen said.

"I know, Gretchen, but the sea has a way of getting into a man's blood. He may give up the sea if you are married, but what if he doesn't?"

Gretchen straightened up and smiled, "We will cross that bridge when we come to it."

Gabe smiled again, "That's the only thing you can do."

It was almost as if he knew that he was being discussed — the marine sentry thudded the deck with the heel of his musket and announced, "Midshipman of the watch, sir."

"Enter," Gabe responded.

"Captain Davy's respects, sir, and the master says we are in for a squall." No then added, "From the way the barometer is acting it may be a big one." Gabe nodded his head.

The watch was being changed and one of the lookouts spoke to Lieutenant Dasher, "Permission to speak to the captain, sir."

Dasher asked, "Did you see something?"

Captain Davy heard the exchange and came over before the lookout could answer. "What is it, Stevens?"

"I've kept my eye on *Active*, sir. It seems that they've had two floggings since I've been on watch."

"Thank you for your report, Stevens. You did right bringing it directly to my attention."

"Thank you, sir."

"Mr. Dasher, see that Stevens gets a double tot tonight."

Smiling, Dasher replied, "I'm not sure Stevens partakes, Captain."

"Oh, yes sir, I does," Stevens threw out.

Dasher gave the man a friendly slap on the back. Gabe looked on and thought, *that was how it used to be when Davy had commanded* Active. ***Now this...***

Overhead, a flash of lightning made up Gabe's mind. The squall was almost on them. Even if he had *Active* close with the flagship, he couldn't transfer over without risking the lives of the boat crew.

Captain Davy walked over, "You heard sir."

"Aye, David, I did. After the squall passes I intend to go to *Active*. I'll take Dagan and Hex and one of your masters at arms. Unless there's reason to change my mind, I intend to relieve Captain Wooten."

"I don't blame you, sir, but how will it look before a board of inquiry?"

"That may be two years from now," Gabe replied. Gretchen's words came to him. "I'll cross that bridge when the time comes."

***

THE SQUALL HIT WITH a force. A few rolls of thunder were heard, each one closer and louder than the previous until they were almost ear shattering. Flashes of lightning seemed to dance all around *Centaur*. The sails were down to storm sails only, and the weather and lightning were so bad that Davy changed the lookout every thirty minutes and at one point almost halted the watch from going aloft.

Ariel was in the great cabin with Faith, Gretchen and Holly. Nanny held James so tight that he complained. Surprisingly, the rough sea didn't cause any more nausea for Ariel. She was at a point now that morning sickness was gone.

Dagan noticed a bit of water coming in from the stern windows. *They'll need new gaskets soon*, he thought, and wondered how they'd been overlooked. Josh got a towel to help soak up the water.

Hex looked over at Gabe, "You're experiencing one of the benefits of your rank, Sir Gabe."

"How's that, Jake?"

"You are in here where it is warm and mostly dry. Poor old Captain Davy is on the quarterdeck sweating in his tarpaulin and still drenched. Of course, if you'd like to be a little nostalgic, I'm sure he'd enjoy your company."

Gabe smiled, "There'll be a cox'n out there checking to see if I'm needed before I go out."

"Sir Gabe, you'd trust me to do that, not being an officer, as it was?" Hex replied.

Gabe snorted, "That could be your pennant overhead had you wanted to be an officer."

"Nay, Sir Gabe. I'll be content to watch my betters."

Faith and Dagan looked at each other smiling. They'd heard Gabe and Hex's japing more than once. Both of them also knew the only thing that kept Jake Hex from walking his own quarterdeck was his loyalty to Gabe.

It was this loyalty that made Dagan feel comfortable leaving Gabe. Walking a quarterdeck and seeing lieutenants jump when he growled would be something he'd miss. But Betsy was worth more than all the ships in the Royal Navy.

***

THE SQUALL WAS STILL pounding the ships and the sea when it was time for the evening meal. There was no way fires could be lit to cook with the ship taking the rolls that she was. 'All hands' had to be called more than once to keep the storm sails on *Centaur*. The men were not only soaked when they'd returned from doing the captain's bidding, but not a hammock was dry, either. Water dripped from the men's clothes until the deck fairly sloshed as the ship rolled. The worst thing was, at least in Stevens' mind, they had to forego the rum ration, and he had a double tot coming to him.

No Stanhope walked through one of the compartments where the men were sitting with their heads hanging down. He quipped to a senior hand, "I wish to God I had my hands on that damn lieutenant who talked me into going to sea. Every day is a different adventure," he said. "Well, Brown, I'd stick this adventure up his broad arse."

The men laughed and a few of them slapped him on the back as he passed them. When he was out of hearing, Brown said, "That un's a good one. We were being shot at from high on the hill. It was on Saint Kitts, it was. Shots were pouring all around us with this Frog officer telling 'is men to pour it on. Men were falling all about. Young No takes a wounded man's musket and jumps up on some rocks. Balls were flying all about him. He takes his aim at the Frog and puts one in 'is chest, 'e did. Said 'e was tired of that damn man, he was. Cool as ye please...bang. When the Frog officer fell, we put it on those Frenchies. Should have made Mr. No an officer right then, but they didn't. There was no medal either, and his grandfather is an Earl as it were." Some of the men already knew the story, but with the storm blowing the legend of Mr. No grew.

Stevens said, "That's all fine and good, but I still wish that we'd gotten our rum ration."

"Up yer arse, Stevens. You be in such good standing wid his 'onour, why don't you go tell 'im we'll 'andle the grog. Just give you the key." Everyone started laughing again.

In the commodore's great cabin, Josh found a pastry for little James, which he devoured right away. He offered the women some cheese and cold meat that they didn't decline. They each took a glass of wine, including Nanny and Gretchen.

The squall lasted through the night, with the last of the rain ending just before dawn. At dawn, much to Gabe's relief, all the ships were on station or close.

The lookout called down as soon as it was light, "Signal from *Active* frigate. Permission to close with flag."

***

Gabe had the squadron continue under easy sail while he boarded *Active*. Lieutenant Standley welcomed his commodore on board. Dagan and Hex came on board as well. Gabe knew that he'd get more from those two than from anyone he talked too. In the captain's cabin, Gabe leaned against the desk.

"When did you notice the captain was missing, Lieutenant?" Gabe inquired.

"I don't know exactly when he went missing, Commodore. I last saw him in the middle watch. I was speaking to Mr. Zachy, the master, about putting a safety rope on the helmsman. The captain yelled to me, 'You have the deck, Mr. Standley.'" the lieutenant answered Gabe.

"You were not the officer on deck?"

"No, sir, Lieutenant York was."

"Where was York?" Gabe asked.

The lieutenant replied, "The gunner sent word that we had some lashings loose on the two forward guns. I sent York and Midshipman Swanson to check things out. Swanson was back soon, saying they were going to need help. I sent Swanson to roust out the next watch. I then went forward to make sure that we didn't lose a gun in the gale, or worse."

"So you left the quarterdeck?"

"Yes, sir. The master was there. He'd been with Captain Davy and I had no reason to doubt that he'd handle whatever came up," the lieutenant said.

"His kind usually can," Gabe admitted, knowing Zachy as he did.

The lieutenant continued, "Once the guns were secured, I came back to the quarterdeck. The captain's servant, Peevey, usually woke the captain each morning so I didn't send for him for quarters. As dawn was breaking and he didn't show up, I went below to his cabin. Peevey said that he wasn't in his sleeping compartment and he thought that the captain was on deck. It seems that the captain's cot hadn't been slept in."

"Do you have any idea what happened to the captain, Lieutenant?" Gabe asked.

"Idea, sir? No sir, but I'd guess that he went over the side," the lieutenant replied.

"Is there anyone on board the ship who may have hated the captain enough for foul play," Gabe inquired.

The lieutenant smiled, "Just about anyone you talked to, sir."

"Including you, Lieutenant?"

"Yes, sir, especially me. I was on board when Captain Davy was our commander, sir. I saw what Wooten was doing to our ship."

"Did you hold a grudge?"

"Yes, sir."

Well, the man didn't lie, Gabe thought. "I understand that you had two floggings yesterday. What were the offenses?" Gabe asked.

"The first offense was a man that laughed, and had a chew in his mouth. Tobacco leaked from his mouth and onto the deck before he could catch it. He was flogged for spitting on the deck. The second offense came when a bosun's mate refused to lay on the cat to the captain's satisfaction. We almost had a mutiny then, but the master intervened, saying that a storm was upon us."

Gabe then asked, "Did you question either of those men?"

"No, sir," the lieutenant responded.

"Why?" Gabe inquired.

"Off the record, sir?" the lieutenant asked. Gabe nodded his head. "Because I was sure that anyone I asked would have an alibi, sir. So why ask."

Gabe nodded, "For the record, Lieutenant, it's my belief that the captain was lost in the storm. I will want a statement from you, the master, and the two helmsmen. It would be best to have the good doctor take their statements, if they can't write. Also, have him take Peevey's statement as well. I will also require a statement from Lieutenant York and Midshipman Swanson, you said?"

"Yes, Sir Gabe. The gunner and...put Fisher down, sir. He was the marine guard and he can swear the captain never went to his cabin."

"Good, let his officer take his statement. Captain Davy speaks highly of you, Lieutenant. I'm going to allow you to remain as first lieutenant. I can see that you've done your duty. One more thing, Lieutenant, the punishment book, where is it?"

"The captain kept that on him at all times, sir, almost like it was an appendage," the lieutenant said.

Gabe nodded but didn't speak. He then said, "Thank you, Lieutenant."

Gabe talked with Hex and Dagan, after they were back on board the flagship. Hex started his report to Gabe, "I think the lashings on the gun were loosened to draw the officers away from the quarterdeck. York will not put it in writing, though, but he checked them before the squall hit."

"What about Zachy?" Gabe asked.

"Besides being deaf, he was busy with the compass and the wheel," Hex responded.

"So what happened?"

"I believe a bosun and carpenter's mate, both who were flogged earlier that day, threw the captain overboard," Dagan replied.

"What happened to the punishment book?" Gabe inquired.

"I think Peevey did that," Dagan said. "He probably threw it out the stern windows."

Gabe then asked, "And the men who were flogged?"

"They were last seen at ten p.m. They were both given an anodyne," Hex said.

"Did they take it?" Gabe inquired.

"The doctor doesn't know for sure, but they were both in sick bay at ten p.m. But who can say after that." Hex offered.

"So you think it was them, the two petty officers," Gabe asked.

"Off the record?" Dagan asked. Gabe nodded and Dagan continued, "I know it was. The captain's tobacco pouch with his initials on it was in one of their coat pockets, which was hanging on a rack by the sick bay door."

How careless, Gabe thought. "Where is the pouch now?"

"It fell over the side, I'm afraid," Hex replied.

"Damn shame," Gabe said.

CHAPTER SIX

"CAPTAIN LAQUA IS HERE, Sir Gabe," Josh said.

"Good," Gabe said. The women had all gathered topside while Gabe attended to his business. "Morning, Ron," Gabe greeted Laqua.

"Sir Gabe."

"Ron, I'm sure that you've heard Captain Wooten disappeared over the side of the ship in the recent storm."

"Yes, sir," Laqua responded.

"I'm making you captain, pending the approval of the Admiralty, and putting you in command of the frigate, *Active*."

"Sir Gabe!"

Gabe waved down anything else that Laqua might have said. "There's no one who deserves it more or who I trust more. I make one recommendation, though; take your servant with you. I don't trust Peevey to keep a confidence."

Josh came in, "Sir Gabe, Lieutenant Dasher is here."

Laqua smiled and said, "He gets *Nimble*." Gabe nodded his head in the affirmative. Laqua continued, "He'll do a good job. We are old friends."

When Dasher was taken to *Nimble*, the sentry called out, "Boat Ahoy."

Hex, who was acting as his cox'n shouted back, "*Nimble*."

Damn, that sounded nice, Dasher thought. Hopefully, he would not cause the commodore any reason to regret his decision.

On board *Active*, acting Captain Ronald Laqua read himself in. After reading his orders, he addressed the officers and crew. "I've known most of you since we set out to take the Silver Galleons from the Dons. I've drunk the beer and shared the women of Playa Potrero." The crew all cheered him. "I was present when *Active* stood broadside to broadside with our enemy. They're gone and we're still here." Another cheer went up. "I know this proud ship has seen some dark days." The crew hung their heads at this comment. "But there will be no more," Laqua said, and repeated, "No more. Today is a new day. My methods are much like Sir Gabe's, as were Captain Davy's. We both were trained by Sir Gabe, our commodore. I will tell you when it comes to running this ship — I will be as strict as any captain who maintains a crack frigate...but I'm fair. I love to hear singing, but you would rather hear a tomcat on the prowl than to hear me. So when there's a time for singing, ring out. I also love the sound of laughter. You only hear laughter on a happy ship. I'll tell you something else. I came up through the ranks. I can smell a shirker all the way from the stern clear to the bow. So don't try to pull one over on me."

Someone shouted, "Ye 'ears that, Foster." The crew laughed again.

"I wish to see the officers and warrants in my cabin in one hour," Laqua said. The crew cheered again.

Gabe looked at Captain Davy, "You hear that?"

"Aye!"

"I don't know what Laqua is saying, but, at least, for now he's won them back over. In one way, I'm glad that Wooten was lost in the storm," Gabe admitted.

"Now, you won't have someone pointing a finger at you," Davy responded. "Who can blame the elements? Certainly not the ones who got the sod the billet."

"You're a good friend, David," Gabe said.

"Aye, and so are you, Sir Gabe."

***

NORFOLK! THE NUMBER OF people gathered to see the ships, that at one time would have caused wholesale panic, was an impressive sight. Near the front of the group, was two figures that Gabe and Dagan recognized right away.

Dagan put his hand on Gabe's shoulder, "I will see you before you sail. I'd like for us to go see Uncle Andre in Petersburg, if possible. If Betsy will have me, there will be a wedding soon. Beyond that, I don't intend to be available much."

"I wish you the best, Uncle," Gabe said. Then as an afterthought, he said, "I'm sure that you have enough money."

Dagan smiled, "Aye, in gold and silver coin."

Gabe thought, *no doubt from the Andalucia*, but didn't say it. He'd seen two burly bosun mates struggle with one of Dagan's two chests. Calling Midshipman Stanhope, Gabe told him to see if Faith was ready to go ashore. He winked at No and said, "If the captain has no objection you can assist the cox'n with Dagan's chest." In truth, he had already mentioned it to Captain Davy, but wanted No to go through the proper channels to prevent the appearance of favoritism. Something he'd had a hard time getting over to Faith and Gretchen.

Hex had Gabe's barge in the water and manned. Faith was soon on deck and No was helping her into a bosun's chair. Once situated, she was lifted up and over the side, and let down into the waiting barge. Gretchen was next and her hands lingered overly long on No's shoulders.

Oaks, the bosun, cleared his throat and said, 'Let's be about it, Mr. Stanhope, me lads have much to do."

No smiled and Gretchen grabbed at the ropes as she was quickly hauled up and over to the barge. No scrambled over the side and was there to help her out of the bosun's chair.

Dagan's two chests went next. He had already gone through the entry port and down the battens, so he was in the barge when the chests were lowered. Gabe, not caring for appearances, took little James, put him on his back, and with James' little hands holding onto his father's neck, they went down the side of the ship. Once at the barge, Hex took James. The little man waved to the men up on the ship's deck, causing them to cheer the commodore's little sailor. Faith smiled as did Gabe.

Once they were on shore, while Gabe was shaking General Manning's hand, Dagan went straight to Betsy. "If you'll still have me, Betsy, I've come to make you my bride."

Betsy was in his arms and heedless of the onlookers, she said, "Yes, I'm yours." The kiss was long and passionate.

Faith had never seen Dagan so happy, and tears of joy came to her eyes. Gretchen caring naught for protocol grasped No's hand and gave it a squeeze.

Captain Davy was there shortly afterwards, and introductions were made even though he'd met General Manning some years ago. The two transports had anchored and boats were plying back and forth bringing the former prisoners of war on shore. One of General Manning's army captains and *Centaur's* second lieutenant listed each of the former prisoners in a book.

Several carriages were lined up to provide transportation for them, and wagons were there also, to carry their belongings to the lodging that had been set up.

"Sir Gabe," General Manning spoke, "while duty makes it necessary for us to remain here until the exchange is complete, perhaps your family would find it more comfortable at my home."

"Thank you, General," Gabe replied.

A wagon was whistled up so that Hex and No could load Dagan's chest, and then the two climbed on board and followed the Manning carriage home.

Once the family had left, General Manning spoke to Gabe and Captain Davy, "I have one of your naval officers here recovering from wounds that he received after his ship and another one was attacked by two much larger ships and sunk."

"After the peace treaty was signed?" Gabe asked.

"I'm afraid so," the general responded.

Captain Troy Skidmore slumped in a carriage. His head only had a small bandage now, where at one time his entire head had been bandaged up trying to protect his scalp, which had been nearly torn loose from his skull. His arm was in a sling and his britches leg was split where his badly burned leg was still bandaged. Two people were in the carriage with him, a nurse and his cox'n, Finch. The man miraculously came through the action, if that was what it could be called; slaughter was more like it, without injury.

"They are coming, Captain," Finch warned.

Troy tried to sit up a little straighter. Gabe saw the pain in the man's face and quickly realized that he'd not recovered from his ordeal.

General Manning made the introductions, and Captain Skidmore quickly gave a concise report of the events. "I've never seen such a ship that attacked *Ferret*," Skidmore said. "Finch, my cox'n, is an old tarpaulin and he felt it was not unlike a xebec, like the Moors use, only much larger. The cannons were twenty-four pounders. Carronades, I'm sure. However, Sir Gabe, there is no doubt that damnable frigate that attacked *Spitfire* was a Spanish heavy frigate, a thirty-eight or larger. I only had time for a glance you understand."

Manning interjected, "The captain of one of our merchant ships saw the debris in the water, so he looked about, finding only Captain Skidmore and Finch."

"Of course, had we not been on a hatch cover, the sharks would have gotten us," Troy said. "Finch used a boarding pike, as it was, on a couple of sharks."

Captain Davy had so far been silent. "Captain Baskins, of the *Spitfire*, was a good officer, a fine seaman. Lord Anthony had him take the lieutenant's exam, Gabe."

The momentary lapse in formality let Gabe know that Davy was taking the news hard. Two frigates sunk with only two survivors...*a damnable loss, and while at peace*.

"We've sent a report to the admiral on Bermuda," Captain Skidmore volunteered.

"Did those ships fly any colors?" Gabe asked.

"No sir," Troy replied.

"Begging your pardon, Commodore, no flag flew, but they were Dons, they were," Finch said. "They sailed right by us and I could hear their chatter. They were Dons alright. There's no doubt in my mind."

Gabe looked at Finch, a man near forty years old, he'd guess, who had been on board Royal Navy ships nearly as long as Gabe had been alive. He'd know, Gabe had no doubt, the man would now. "Take care of your captain, cox'n. I'll have you back on your own quarterdeck before long." *Now why in the hell did I say that*, Gabe wondered. The man would have to face a court martial for losing his ship. He'd do his best to help him, Gabe decided. There was not much that could be expected of a ship with nine pounders facing twenty-four pound carronades. He was lucky that his cox'n got him on a hatch cover.

Noticing the nurse, Gabe spoke to her, "Madam, it may well be beneficial to Captain Skidmore's future if his doctor would write a report detailing each of the captain's injuries and how severe they were."

"He will be glad to do it, Sir," the nurse replied.

"Good," Gabe said, "some reports are often very sketchy at best."

"These will be very detailed and specific, Sir. The good doctor is my brother." The nurse saying this took Troy's hand. Gabe smiled, another American woman with desires for a British officer.

"I will have Doctor Honeycutt visit with you as well," Davy volunteered.

Theoretically, this business with the Spanish raiders was the business of the admiral in Bermuda. However, Gabe had a feeling that it wouldn't stay that way.

CHAPTER SEVEN

A huge welcome home feast was planned for that next evening. It was not only a welcome home but also a fond farewell to many of the British prisoners of war. Most of whom were former army officers and soldiers. A few of the soldiers had made friends, started families, and were given permission to remain in the United States. The officers had given their parole and had become good friends with their Yankee cousins, a few of them had also married. The remaining British prisoners were ready to see England again but their hearts were heavy at leaving their friends.

The streets were filled with people, and spirits were being taken, not only in the inn and taverns, but the jovial mood had spilled over into the streets. Dagan and Betsy were taking No back to the ship. He'd been able to spend most of the day and afternoon with Gretchen but being conscientious he knew that he needed to report back to the ship. He reported to Captain Davy before leaving to see if he wished him to carry any messages to the first lieutenant.

"Yes, I do, Mr. Stanhope," Davy said. He then took out the address to the doctor's house where Captain Skidmore was being treated. "Let the good Doctor Honeycutt know that we have a captain who was injured in battle staying at this address. I would appreciate his calling on him when it is convenient." He then wrote a quick note and folded it. "Give this to the first lieutenant please."

"Aye, aye, Captain," No replied.

Davy was happy that No had reported that he was going back to the ship. Some would have waited until they were ordered to go back. No, by not taking advantage of Gabe's trust and friendship, had just gone up another notch on his captain's list. With Lieutenant Dasher being placed on board Nimble as captain, a vacancy was open for a lieutenant on Centaur. Davy had not automatically filled it with No, even though he was the senior mid, because by doing so, it would have cut down on his freedom to spend time with Gretchen. Once they left port would be time enough.

Dagan and Betsy dropped No off at the waterfront, where a boat took him the short distance to the flagship. The carriage then started back to the Manning house. Dagan suddenly called to the coachman, "Driver stop. Stop please."

Dagan jumped from the coach before it stopped. Standing in the door was a familiar looking figure. The man's long mane was snow white. "Frosty! Frosty," Dagan called.

Hearing his name above the din of the people in the tavern, the old man turned and looked. He squinted and looked again. "Be you that Britisher that I took traipsing through the woods to yer uncle's," the man asked.

"The same," Dagan replied. Looking at the man, who had guided him and a doctor named Caleb through enemy lines to his uncle's house at the beginning of the war, he seemed little changed. He had on the same buckskin clothes, the same moccasins on his feet, and the same drooping mustache and shapeless hat.

"I, by gawd, do remember you," Frosty said. "Did you find yer kin in one piece?"

"Aye, we did, thanks to you," Dagan replied.

"Naw, I just led you to Petersburg," Frosty responded.

Dagan introduced Frosty to Betsy, who greeted the old woodsman pleasantly. "My kin," Dagan said, "is a grown man now. He's is charge of all those ships that you see flying the British flag."

"I 'spose that's good as long as he hasn't killed no Americans, not many least ways," Frosty said.

"No, very few Americans," Dagan responded. "They were mostly French and Spanish."

"I never did cotton to any snail eaters myself," Frosty replied.

"Come with us," Dagan offered. "I want you to meet Gabe and his wife. She is an American."

"Do tell! No wonder he was particular who he kilt." Frosty had a tankard in his hand. He drained the ale in it and then tossed it over to the tavern wall. "They'll fetch it in before long." Frosty eyed Betsy, as he was getting in the coach, "You shore getting' you a plum purty woman, boy. What was the name again?"

"Dagan."

"No, not yours, hers," Frosty said.

"Betsy," Dagan replied.

"Well, Betsy, I guess you know what yer getting yourself in fer. I do have to say what I remember of yer man, he'd do to ride the river with," Frosty said.

Once they got to the Manning's house, Dagan introduced Frosty to everyone. Gabe took to the man right away.

"I'll say one thing fer you British, you sure do pick purty gals," Frosty said. Hearing Faith speak, Frosty took her hand and said, "Gurl, you sho' 'nuff come from God's neck of the woods. Be it Georgia?"

"Close, Beaufort, South Carolina," Faith answered.

"I'd say that'd be close enough. I'm right proud to have met you," Frosty responded.

Before Frosty left, Dagan invited him to the wedding. Gabe then mentioned that they'd planned on visiting his uncle in Petersburg again and would like to hire him as a guide.

"Shore," Frosty said. "It won't be nary as much fun as when I took Dagan, since there ain't no army patrols to dodge." This got a laugh from the group.

When Frosty was leaving, Dagan slipped a coin into his hands, "For old times."

"Generous, right generous you are. I'll fetch up with you and learn when yer wedding is to be."

***

THE BAPTIST PREACHER WHO performed Betsy and Dagan's wedding had known the Manning family since Betsy was a child. She had often told him of Dagan, but secretly the minister had his doubts as to when the woman would realize her dreams, but they had come true. Three short days after Dagan's arrival, he and Betsy were married. The modest church was packed as the minister looked out over the largest number of people who'd ever filled his pews, as he performed the ceremony.

Once the wedding was over and the reception finally ended, Frosty took the newlyweds up into the tidewater area, where on a bluff, with the sea crashing ashore, they spent a week in a cottage that Betsy's mother's family owned. It was a small cottage, and once it was known that Dagan had arrived, it had been fully stocked.

Frosty left two horses in a small stable with a paddock in case they wanted to go riding. A small two room shack had been built to the side of the cottage. It was so new the wood still had an odor. Once she'd heard that the prisoner exchange would take place, Betsy had set things in motion. She knew that when the ship with the prisoners arrived, Dagan would be on it.

Later that night, with only one candle lit, its small flame created a dancing shadow on the wall near the bed. A tub was in the room and the servant girl had heated some water, filled the tub and scattered rose petals over the water and then left.

After a very long and passionate kiss the newlyweds' fingers fumbled with snaps and buttons as they undressed each other. Then splashing a bit of water over the side, they bathed each other, lips kissing, fingers touching and exploring each other's body.

"I've longed for this moment every day since you left," Betsy whispered.

"As have I," Dagan replied, speaking softly.

"I'm no longer a young girl," Betsy said.

"I was looking for a woman, not a girl," Dagan replied.

Betsy smiled and said, "And I have my man."

After their bath was complete, Dagan marveled at how beautiful Betsy's nude body was. Her body defied her years. Her breasts stood proud and erect, her nipples inviting him to kiss and caress them. Her stomach was flat, and her bottom perfectly rounded.

"You have the body of a goddess," Dagan whispered as he kissed her neck from behind.

"I've tried to keep fit to please you, plus I've never been with child. When a woman has a child, it makes big changes in her body."

"I'd love you no matter the shape of your body," Dagan whispered as his hand reached around his wife cupping her breasts and pulling her against him.

She reached behind and touched his manhood. "I believe you've become excited," Betsy proclaimed.

"I've been excited since I saw you at the waterfront," Dagan replied.

"And I you," Betsy said.

Dagan moved around his wife and lifted her in his

arms. He carried her the few feet to the bed. As she held on to him, Dagan raked the comforter back with one hand and then placed Betsy down on the bed's cool sheets.

"Come to me, my husband. Shower me with your love."

Dagan smiled, and then his lips closed with hers, a hand cupping a breast while the other hand held the back of her head. Betsy's arms were around Dagan, pulling him on top of her, and then the years of pent up desires flowed rapidly. The rhythm of their breathing grew quicker and quicker until the dam burst and their passion flooded forth. They were both wet with sweat as they collapsed in a tangle of entwined arms and legs. They slept the contented sleep of lovers.

When nature called, it was not yet light outside. When they came back to bed, it was Betsy who was on top. In moments the flames of desire quickly grew out of control. Afterwards, they slept until the sun was high in the morning sky and the aroma of coffee found its way to the bedroom. Betsy got up and went over to the tub. She sponged off in its cool water.

Seeing his wife shiver, Dagan said, "Come back to bed, I'll warm you up."

Betsy smiled and said, "That's what I'm afraid of."

CHAPTER EIGHT

The Spanish warships *La Cazadora* and *La Tigresa* cleared the harbor at Santiago de Cuba. The reception of the ships in Havana had not been what either captain had expected. Havana was a long way from Madrid, and the two ships' captains broodingly accepted the offer of using Santiago. The island's governor seemed to resent the activities of the two ships.

"You must understand," the governor said, addressing the ships' captains, "If we are attacked because of your activities, the island will fall. You will sail away and we shall be at the mercy of the British Royal Navy." The two captains snorted at the governor's words. *Coward*, they both thought.

Capitán de Fragata Juan Alvarado and Mateo Monterio no longer wore the uniform of Spain, and neither did any of their crew. However, their ships were as Spanish as were their language, with only a few of the men speaking poor English. Both of the captains were utterly ruthless, which was why they were chosen for the task at hand.

Spain had, at one time, held a vast empire in America. However, several possessions had been lost during the Colonies' revolution against England. Spain had secretly supported the Colonies before openly becoming allies. Spain now had little to show for their allegiance. Spain's main goal then was to distract the British in the Caribbean, so much so, that they'd pull their ships away from Gibraltar and Menorca, freeing up the Mediterranean. But due to the Peace Treaty, it could not be done openly. Spain still wanted to provoke the British, but was not ready to wage an all out war again. They had not yet recovered from losses for siding with the French during the Seven Year War, nor from siding with the French again as allies to the Colonials. It would take time to amass a fleet and army...not only time, but money.

The French were in open rebellion. Thousands of men, women, and even children were being put to death. Some were already calling the French Revolution the first born child of the American Revolution. The Monarchy and the French government were taxing their people to pay for assisting America against the British.

When Benjamin Franklin preached of overthrowing the British king and open rebellion against England, the French people listened. The American, in his shabby homespun clothes, hit a common accord with the French people. It was inevitable that the French would soon follow suit. The tumult in France was just beginning, but it played directly in the minds of the Spanish. If France went to war as expected, the British would find themselves hard-pressed to protect all their possessions. Gibraltar and other lost islands would become vulnerable to assault.

The *La Cazadora* and *La Tigresa* would for now, as one termed it, tickle the tiger's arse, so much so that England would be forced to show its claws. *La Cazadora*, the *Huntress*, was an unusual ship. She was a xebec – frigate. She was more suited for the coast off of Algeria. But Capitán de Fragata Juan Alvarado loved his ship. During his time commanding her, she'd never lost a battle. He'd convinced his superiors that he could sail his strange ship to the Caribbean and even into the Atlantic Ocean and do a better job than any other. He had impressed his superiors and here he was. He'd gotten the support he and *La Tigresa* needed, even if Cuba's spineless governor did it, fearing Alvarado more than the British.

The *Huntress* was a six hundred ton ship. Her crew consisted of three hundred twenty-five officers and men. She carried twenty-two eighteen pounder guns, four eight pounder guns, and six twenty-four pounder carronades, two forward and four on the quarterdeck. The weight of these smashers had been the difference in several battles. It was rare that a ship could match its weight in metal.

The *Tigress* was a big forty gun frigate, but it only carried eighteen pounders with six pounders on the quarterdeck and forecastle. The *Tigress* was a force in her own right, but teamed up with the *Huntress*, they were a deadly pair. The two ships sailed to the south looking for any British ships that presented, but their destination was the distant island of Tobago. They would stand off and blast away at the island's defenses. Nearly every plantation owner had installed cannons to protect themselves, but the main objective for the two Spanish ships would be Fort King George. It had been built in 1770, with numerous heavy guns pointing out to sea, but with the peace treaty, they would not be expecting a bombarding. After that, they'd see what the third ship in their small force recommended.

The third ship was a small merchant vessel with enough trade goods to make its disguise look believable. The fat, jovial, short Angel Santiago was the consummate spy. He'd just returned from Trinidad and Tobago. While Juan Alvarado didn't like the little man giving him orders, he realized that should anything go wrong, it would be Santiago's fault. He would be the man who answered to Madrid. Alvarado could live with that.

***

ALL WAS AS IT should be outside the lazy little town of Scarborough. Soldiers at the fort relieved the watch. Since it was peace time, the lieutenant in charge of the fort was busy trying to impress a planter's daughter of his vast responsibility. The sergeant, who was as everyone knew, actually the man in charge, took his responsibilities more to heart than the lieutenant did. But years of idleness had even caused the sergeant to be less demanding than he'd once been. Tonight, he'd gotten a letter from his wife in East Sussex. He only had six more months on this Godforsaken little island and then he'd be due to return to England. He had already spent twenty-eight years in the army. He'd do sixteen months at the barracks when he got home and then retire, if he didn't die of boredom first.

The lieutenant had just walked past a sentry on the outer wall, still trying to impress his girl. The sentry, a private, saw the two ships reduce sail. "Begging the lieutenant's pardon, sir. Those two ships are acting more strangely than any ships that I've seen before."

The lieutenant rolled his eyes at the girl and then turned to the private, "Where...what ships?"

"There," the private answered, pointing out to sea.

The lieutenant looked in time to see a long burst of flame leap from the sides of the ships. The ground around him seemed to jump beneath his feet. As he was hurled over the fort's walls, he heard the thunder of the ships' guns and saw the private and the girl suddenly disappear as if they'd never been there.

The sergeant shoved his letter in his pocket and shouted out orders to man the guns. The few soldiers on duty rushed to the magazine to get the powder and shot. Somebody had the bugle blaring, which was the alarm that the fort was being attacked. *Damn fool,* the sergeant thought, *if the roar of cannons doesn't get their attention, that bugle won't.*

Balls from the ships were raining down all around the fort. One ball hit a mortar, and now there was only a crater remaining where the gun had been. Soldiers were flooding in through the gate and a gunner indicated that their gun was ready.

The sergeant said, "Aim well. Remember you're aiming downhill and then fire at will."

Screams and an explosion were heard to the sergeant's left. A ball from the ships hit a cannon just as it was being loaded. The other guns were firing now and one ball landed beside a ship, while another ball put a hole through a sail, and then it was over.

The colonel came up to the sergeant, "Where is Lieutenant Johnson?"

The sergeant replied, "I don't know, he was by the wall when the first shells hit."

"You had no warning, Sergeant?" the colonel asked.

Before the sergeant could speak, a private spoke, "A sentry was pointing out the ships when they fired. I'm afraid the lieutenant, his girl, and the sentry were all caught in the first blast."

"Very well, son, good report. Sergeant, get a detail together and let me know the butcher's bill."

"Yes, sir," the sergeant responded.

The colonel then asked, "Did anybody see a flag?"

"They were not flying one when they sailed away," the sergeant said.

"Damme," the colonel hissed. "Are we at war again and no one thought to inform us."

The governor was soon there and the colonel reported, "Sixteen wounded, seven dead that we know of, including a lady guest of Lieutenant Johnson."

"That will be Abercombie's daughter," the governor

said, hanging his head. "She had just turned sixteen."

"We lost four guns—three cannons and a mortar," the Colonel said. He then looked at the governor and asked, "Are we at war again, sir?"

Shaking his head, the governor replied, "If we are, Colonel, this is the first that I've heard of it."

The sergeant noticed that his sleeve was bloody. A piece of shrapnel had sliced his arm muscle. It had bled a good deal, but while it burned, there was little real pain. The colonel sent him to the doctor to be looked at. As the sergeant walked, he thought, *I bet that I don't get relieved on time now, damn their black-hearted souls.*

CHAPTER NINE

THE TRIP TO PETERSBURG was much different than Dagan's previous trip with Frosty. They were able to take the main roads, which made the trip both easier and faster.

"Taint near the fun howsoever," Frosty declared. "Dodging those war time patrols was half the fun." He then entertained Faith, Betsy, and Gretchen with tales of slipping guns and powder through the British patrols, often passing so close he could hear them talking. "They just didn't have no woods learning," Frosty declared. "They blocked roads and bridges when not a hundred feet away was a perfect trail to creek crossings."

Dagan smiled at the old man's tales. Bypassing the patrols hadn't been so easy as Frosty made it out to be, but he'd gotten them through and that was all that counted.

The group had traveled the eighty miles to Petersburg at a leisurely pace. It was late morning on the third day when Dagan recognized the stone fence leading up to his uncle's place. "We are almost there," he informed everyone.

Gabe was excited to meet his grandfather's brother and his great uncle. They saw the roof of the barn and then the house. Before they got to the yard, the family dogs started barking, alerting everyone that guests were arriving. As the dog stood his ground, barking and growling, Frosty spit a mouthful of tobacco juice at the hound, hitting him on the nose. The dog yelped and then turned in a circle and started to bark again. A voice called to the dog to hush. As the lead carriage drew up in the yard, chickens scattered out of the way.

A man was coming down the steps, waving as he did so. Jubal, the boy who had accompanied Dagan on his quest to find Gabe, was now a man. Behind him on the porch was a girl with blondish hair. Her dress stopped just below her knees and she was barefoot.

"Dagan," Jubal shouted. "I'd just told Hannah that you'd be here soon."

The memory of Andre's words flooded back to Dagan. 'He's got the gift, same as you.' Hannah was coming down the steps.

"We were going to check on some fish traps," Jubal volunteered. "That's why she is dressed so."

Before Dagan could speak, he heard a shout. It was Andre. He was walking from the barn, drying his hands on a towel. Suspenders held up his britches and his sleeves were rolled up. He wore no hat and his black hair had lots of gray about his ears. A big smile creased his tan, weather beaten face. Greetings were made all around.

Gabe said, "I've always wanted to meet you, Uncle Andre. I told mother that since we were coming to Norfolk, I wouldn't leave until we had visited."

"I'm glad that you did, son. I've wanted to meet you as well. How is my sister?" Andre asked.

"She has recently remarried," Gabe told his uncle. "She is now Lady Stanhope. She married an earl."

"My Lord!" Andre exclaimed.

"Maria and her husband are planning to come visit you in a few months," Dagan said.

"We would enjoy that," Andre and Jubal said in unison.

"Where's old Kawliga?" Dagan asked.

"He's about, we have several mares that are ready to foal. He wants to bring them up and put them in one of the paddocks near the barn."

"They don't give birth in the pasture?" Gabe asked.

"They do and have for years, but if they are close we can check on them better. We can also make sure that some critter doesn't get after them." While the pastures around the farm seemed very large, the woods were still in view.

Gretchen and Hannah were chatting and walked inside. Andre turned to Betsy, "So you are the woman who stole my nephew's heart."

"Gabe's wife is also an American, Uncle," Dagan volunteered.

"'Peers they's both got more than passin' brains," Frosty said. "They both got sense enough to take American wives." This created a chuckle from the group.

The group walked up and spread out on the front porch. Before long, Gretchen came back out barefoot, wearing tied up pants. "I'm going with Hannah and Jubal," she announced.

"If Becky could only see you now," Faith said with a chuckle.

"I'll bet that she's never been so relaxed," Gabe said.

Dagan replied, "We might not get her to go back with us."

"Yes, we will," Faith responded. No isn't here." They explained to Andre then who No was.

For a week, Gabe and his family stayed with Uncle Andre. His old friend, Caleb, and his wife, Kitty, came over, and they even brought Caleb's ape, Mr. Jewels. The ape was almost entirely gray now and he didn't stray far from either Caleb or Kitty. There were no children with them, which Gabe thought odd. Especially after the way Kitty played with little James.

Gabe mentioned it to Faith that night, and she said, "Kitty has had two pregnancies, but she lost both of them before three months."

The next morning at breakfast, Gabe noticed that Dagan and Jubal were not present. "They were up at first light and left together," Andre said. The day wore on and Gabe was feeling a bit uneasy about Dagan and Jubal being gone so long. He walked in to the kitchen where the women were. They were cooking figs to turn into preserves. Gretchen was in awe. She'd led a very sheltered life and now realized it. Gabe was suddenly glad that they had brought the girl with them. She and Hannah had quickly become friends. Yesterday, in another pair of britches, she was riding with Hannah, only the horses were bareback and she sat straddled on the horse. She thoroughly enjoyed the ride and freedom from the dress and shoes.

Gabe made his way to the barn where Andre had gone. As he entered the barn, he saw Kawliga. Asking if he'd seen Dagan and Jubal, the old Indian grunted. "Dagan teach Jubal the gift and the old ways. They come back tomorrow." Satisfied, Gabe worried no more.

The women went into Petersburg later that day and returned with several packages. Among them were two pair of britches and shirts that fit Gretchen. Neither her parents nor No will recognize her as the same girl, Gabe had joked.

Dagan and Jubal were there at breakfast the next day. It was Sunday, so after breakfast they went to the little church not far from Andre's farm. The next morning as they prepared to leave, Andre led two horses out to the carriages, a mare and a gelding.

"They were twins at birth, so they should stick together," Andre said. Smiling he added, "A wedding gift to Dagan and Betsy. They are from a breed in Spain. The Spanish call them spotted horses but I've also heard the term Appaloosa. I bought the first one, a stallion, from a man in Florida and later bought a mare from a trader short on funds. We now have about twenty. They are very gentle thanks to Hannah, who treats them like pets." Hannah smiled at Andre.

When Dagan hugged Kitty as they were saying their goodbyes, he stepped back and looked at her. He stepped next to her again and placed a hand on her stomach. Stepping back again, he looked at Caleb. "Your wife carries your child. It will be a strong, healthy child."

Tears came to Kitty's eyes as Caleb embraced his wife, with tears on his face now. Everyone cheered. Dagan looked at Hannah then and said, "You will give Andre grandsons." Everyone clapped their hands.

Lying on a blanket that night next to her husband, Betsy asked, "Will we have children?"

"More than you can count, but they will be nieces and nephews. I fear that our time has passed," Dagan replied.

"Will you still love me?" Betsy asked.

"With all that I am," Dagan said, kissing his wife and pulling her close to him.

They made it to Norfolk on Wednesday morning. Gabe went directly to the ship. Hex had stayed at the Mannings' house, getting to know the old general and making sure that he was given the appropriate treatment by the Navy officers. There wasn't an officer who wanted the cox'n to report less than cordial behavior to the commodore.

"It seems strange, Sir Gabe, for us to be doing what we are without Dagan along," Hex said.

"Aye, Jake, but my uncle has devoted his life to me.

It's time that he enjoys his life with his wife," Gabe replied.

Hex responded, "Well, if the weight of that chest means anything, it should be very enjoyable."

Gabe smiled and thought, *how many years had Dagan contributed to his retirement?*

CHAPTER TEN

FOG DRIFTED OVER THE lowlands that lay between Savannah and the South Carolina border. The squadron had weighed anchor and left Norfolk the Monday after returning from visiting Gabe's uncle and family in Petersburg. When they left they carried a few families with them, since Savannah was closer to their home than Norfolk

Captain Troy Skidmore and his cox'n, Peter Finch, sailed with them as well. Doctor Honeycutt felt Troy was at a point where he could safely be brought on board the ship. Doctor Robert Cornish and his wife, after meeting Caleb and Kitty in Norfolk, had decided to return with them to Petersburg.

It had been a sad farewell, as Doctor Cornish had been with Gabe a number of years. But the hardest thing was weighing anchor and not having Dagan at his side. He'd always been there; even from his first memory of his boyhood, Dagan had been at his side. Gabe didn't begrudge his uncle staying. He'd earned it a thousand times over, plus he'd found love. Betsy had waited years for this, as had Dagan, and they were together now.

Gabe, with his arms around Dagan and Betsy, had said with a trembling voice and fighting tears, "May God grant you years of love, health, and happiness together."

Faith cried, telling Dagan how much she loved him. When they made their way to the carriage, Dagan had reached down and scooped up little James, "Uncle Dagan will come visit before long."

It had been a short, uneventful voyage to Savannah. Gabe was able to turn matters over to Davy after the second day, having completed all the required tasks. Following the road to Faith's uncle's house, Gabe was glad that the hired coachman knew the way, as the road was only visible in spots. The horses trotted along seemingly oblivious to the fog. Lanterns had been lit at each of the coach's four corners. They pulled over once to let several wagons traveling together pass over a narrow bridge. While they were waiting, Gabe stepped out of the coach. When he looked back, the lanterns gave the coach an eerie appearance in the thick fog.

When they were to go, Gabe spoke to Faith, "Do you remember when I came to see you and asked your Uncle Gavin for your hand?"

Caroline and Gavin Lacy had taken Faith in after there'd been trouble with her father's brother, Adam Montique. He was a swine and a traitor to both the Colonies and England. Gavin Lacy had been Faith's father's business partner. When Faith had left, he had looked after both Faith's and his plantations.

"Yes, how could I forget it," Faith said. "You, a British naval officer, in a country you were at war with, walked up to the house as if you were on a Sunday stroll." She leaned over and kissed Gabe. "My man had come from the sea to see me...at great risk. Uncle Gavin told me, after you left, that for a man to risk a firing squad to visit a girl was a man he'd respect. You better marry that man first chance you get, he said."

The reunion at the Lacy plantation was as festive as the reception at Petersburg. Gavin Lacy, after shaking Gabe's hand, stood back and looked him over. "You've come a long way since that gangly boy lieutenant who snuck up to the house to see his girl."

Caroline spoke then, "And look at Faith, Gavin. She is a grown woman and a mama, as well."

Faith introduced Gretchen and Gabe introduced Hex. Lum and Nanny needed no introductions. Caroline hugged Nanny and then took little James in her arms.

They were sipping cold sweet tea an hour later when Gavin broached the subject that he knew was on Faith's mind. "Live Oak," he said, meaning Faith's plantation "is doing well. The war had little effect in that area. You've had some good crops and I've put aside a nice sum for you. I kept one-third for my expenses and some cost associated with travel."

"Thank you, Uncle Gavin, but one-third is too little. I want you to have half," Faith said.

"I can't do that, girl," Gavin responded.

"You will, and that's the end to it," Faith exclaimed.

Caroline spoke to her husband, "Tell her, Gavin."

Gavin leaned forward in his rocking chair and grasped Faith's hand where she sat in the swing. "You know, child, that none of our children have survived. You are the closest thing to a relative that we have. You've always been more like a daughter to us anyway."

Caroline broke in and said, "Your mama was my best friend."

"Aye," Gavin agreed. "Thomas, your daddy, and I were business partners in the shipping business. We each bought our plantations when we quit the sea. Faith, your Aunt Caroline and I have decided that when we pass, River View will be yours."

Gabe could see Faith's chin quiver and tears drop from her eyes as she got out of the swing. She knelt down between the two rocking chairs and hugged Gavin and Caroline. On the last porch step, Nanny sat watching little James play in the dark soil.

Gavin looked down and said to Faith, "Who knows, girl, that little man of yours may find the farm more to his liking than the sea."

Gavin Lacy had no idea how true his words would become.

***

CON VALLIN, WAS CAPTAIN of HMS *Ares* of forty-four guns. His assignment was to make a patrol eastward to Puerto Rico, and then southerly to Aruba, Bonaire, and Curacao. The islands lay off the northern coast of Venezuela. Some people were beginning to call them the ABC islands. Those islands were Dutch. He'd sail westerly then toward Nicaragua, and then northerly past Roatan and up to the Grand Caymans. The admiral at the Jamaica station told Con that he'd think it amiss if he didn't spend at least a week with his girl on Grand Cayman.

The Royal Navy dockyard at Port Royal continued to build even though the war with the Colonies had ended. The admiral had said someone in power knows the war with France is probably coming. They also know how important this station is, and therefore, the facility continues to grow and add more services.

The ABC islands had been quiet. There was very little shipping headed for trade with the Dutch islands at that time.

The island of Roatan lay to larboard. The mainmast lookout called down, "Two ships off the coast of yonder island, Cap'n. One is Don frigate, and the other is like I never see'd."

Vallin took a glass from a midshipman. He was not able to see as well as he liked on the quarterdeck, so he went over and climbed up the shrouds. One ship, though it flew no colors, was a Spanish frigate, there was no doubt. The other ship, he looked at long and hard. He watched until she crossed the reef and entered into Port Royal. The island now belonged to the Dons. They had mounted an attack on the British settlers in 1782 by sending a fleet of warships to oust the settlers. To see the two ships entering a Spanish port was not unusual, but to be flying no colors, that was a mystery.

Cautioning his first lieutenant to keep a watchful eye, Captain Vallin went below to a reference library he'd put together over the years. He was about tired of the search when he found a sketch and description of the ship that he was looking for. A xebec, but more than just a xebec, a xebec frigate. It was most unusual in those waters indeed. He made a log entry and made an entry in his daily journal. It was something that he'd certainly report. They'd received word at Jamaica of two small frigates disappearing from Bermuda. Did those strange ships have anything to do with it? He wasn't sure, but something that he'd heard Gabe Anthony say often enough, 'I don't much believe in coincidences.' *Neither does Con Vallin,* he decided.

CHAPTER ELEVEN

Mr. Midshipman Noble 'No' Pride Stanhope watched as the carpenter, Joseph Morales, fashioned a small cot that would swing. It was not unlike the one the commodore and his wife shared. It would keep the little man's bed from having to be anchored to the deck in some fashion. It came to No that it would also keep the little rascal out of Gabe and Faith's bed. Thinking of Gabe and Faith in bed naturally progressed to what it would be like to share the bed with Gretchen. He surely missed the girl.

When Gretchen came back from visiting Uncle Andre in Petersburg, she was full of tales of going barefoot, wearing a male's britches, riding straddle a horse, playing in the creek and other adventures. The tales caused No to second guess his decision to make the Navy a career for a while.

Once they were at sea, it was better, but now they were anchored in the port of Savannah. However, Jake Hex had returned to the ship last evening and talked with Captain Davy. Liberty was being granted by watch and would continue as long as the ships were in port if...the almighty if. If everyone returned on time and stayed out of trouble with their American cousins. Hex was to take a change of traveling clothes for Gabe and Gretchen. He was also to invite Major LoGiudice and Holly, plus Doctor Cook and Jimena to travel to Live Oak in Beaufort, Faith's plantation. Doctor Cook and Jimena were not at their inn, but

Ariel, Captain's Davy's wife did join them.

The trip was near forty miles so they left early in the morning, skirting the marsh, and changing horses at Bluffton, and then to the Port Royal ferry at Broad River. The group arrived at Live Oak just before dark. The overseer, a man that Gavin Lacy had hired, made his way out to meet the new arrivals. Seeing Gavin, the overseer, Mr. Barry Lincoln, walked over. Gavin introduced everyone.

"So this is the lady that owns Live Oak. It's a pleasure to meet you and your family, Mrs. Anthony," the overseer said.

Lum and Nanny made their way to the main house in hopes of renewing old acquaintances. As Gabe and Faith's friends took in the plantation they were amazed. The huge oaks coming down the lane covered the road so it felt like they were in a tunnel barely above their heads. Spanish moss hung low from the trees. The drive made a circle and on each side of the circle were two statues. Each statue with an iron ring attached was used to tie horses.

The front of the house, or better described as 'mansion,' stood before them. Eight white columns held up the balcony on the second floor. The windows were huge. They were so big that a person could walk through one. The house and front porch were set high off the ground. There were ten steps, at least twenty feet wide, leading up to the porch. The house was wood and painted white, but it had been bricked from the ground up to the porch. Scattered about were all sorts of buildings.

Faith was pointing out the barn, the blacksmith's area, the sawmill, and past the sawmill close to the river was the grist mill. Mr. Lincoln smiled and said, "You haven't forgotten anything."

They went up the steps and into the house, and

the first thing that Faith did was go into the sitting room. There on each side of the fireplace was a large painting of her mother and father, and hanging in the center was a painting of Faith. It was done just as she was turning sixteen.

A white woman walked up, having come from the back. Lincoln introduced her, "This is my wife, Martha. She has made sure that things have been maintained in the house, basically as you left them."

Martha counted heads and spoke to a teenage black girl telling her how many there would be for dinner. She then asked about the bedrooms. Hex and No would share a room. Ariel and Gretchen shared one, and then there would be one for each married couple.

After the evening meal, Mr. Lincoln explained, "We rebuilt most of the slave quarters last year."

Gavin broke in then, "The overseer's house needs the same. Barry and Martha have two children, Doris and Sheridan. They're ten and twelve. "

Faith nodded and said, "They are at an age that they need separate bedrooms. Let's make that a priority. In the meantime, this house has more than enough room."

Martha laughed, "We had a storm that tore off most of the roof so we did stay in here several nights."

"I've tried to be a good steward of the land, Mrs. Anthony. We grow corn for food, and livestock, cotton, and tobacco in a few acres, rice and, even though we lost the support of England we still grow about one hundred acres of indigo," the overseer said.

"The textile mills are still running, so I think that you'll see the demand for indigo again," Gabe said.

"We have also put in about seventy acres of different vegetables," Barry said. "What we don't eat, we sell."

"Live Oak was not affected then by the war," Faith said.

"Not much," Barry replied. "There was a battle where we beat the redcoats, but then our army left. The redcoats came back soon after that. A few officers came by seeing the only animals we had was some mules for plowing, and four milk cows. They took a dozen or so chickens and left. They tried to talk the slaves into joining their army but the major was so snobbish that nobody wanted to leave. He held a perfumed handkerchief to his nose the entire time that he was talking to the slaves. He also kept shooing away the kids so nobody wanted to go with him." The depiction that Barry gave created laughter at the table, and realizing what he'd said made the overseer blush.

Gabe, seeing the man turn red, spoke, "We have a few of those in the Navy as well."

Lying in Faith's old bed that night, she turned on her side to face Gabe, "You don't know how many times after I found you, that I would lay in this bed and wonder what it'd be like to have you with me, letting you have your way with me."

Gabe inched closer to Faith, kissed her and whispered, "Let's make your fantasy come true."

Faith said nothing, as she sat up and removed her nightgown. "Ravish me if you will, sailor boy, but I warn you it may prove to be more than you can handle."

"I shall do my best," Gabe responded, as he gently bit a nipple. Faith crushed his head to her, and then laughed. Gabe released the nipple and looked up, "What's so funny?"

Faith smiled and responded, "I can just hear Nanny now. 'Laud child, yo mama would roll over in her grave if she knew how you were acting. You done got ta acting like one of old Master Hindley's tavern wenches, you sho nuff has.'" Gabe was laughing so that Faith put her hand over his mouth and pulled his head back to her breasts.

For the next several days they explored Live Oak from one boundary to another. They caught catfish and went crabbing. They made a trip to Port Royal and to Beaufort, and even took a boat out into the bay shrimping. The last evening at Live Oak, Martha planned a traditional low country treat...Frogmore stew. For many of the guests, it was something they'd never had, nor heard of. It consisted of sausage, shrimp, corn, potatoes, Cajun spice, and on top of it crab meat cooked in little cakes. There was both wine and ale served with the meal. Cider was available but no one touched it.

The planned early departure the next morning was delayed. Barry spoke to the group that morning at the breakfast table, "I fear that your departure may be delayed a day, maybe more."

"Why so?" Gavin asked.

"I believe that we are in for a gully washer," Barry replied.

"A what?" Gabe asked.

"A hard rain," Faith answered. "What you might call a squall at sea."

A crash of lightning and a boom of thunder so loud that it shook the house echoed Faith's description. Gretchen looked over at No and smiled, then under the table, she squeezed his hands. By late that afternoon, the planks leading down to the small dock were under water. The ground back behind the house stood in water. It was now apparent why the main floor of the house was eleven feet off the ground.

The rain was gone the next morning. Gavin, Gabe, and Hex rode down to the ferry at Port Royal. The ferryman had pulled the ferry up, high enough in his yard so that the current wouldn't get to it.

Porter, the ferryman, seeing and recognizing Gavin, said, "It won't be today and likely not tomorrow either. The river is too swollen."

"Well, Gabe, it looks like Faith will have a few more days at home," Gavin said.

***

A CRY FROM ONE of the bedrooms brought Faith and Gabe up in their bed. It came again, though it was not as loud. They got up and, leaving their room, walked down the hall. The other guests were at their bedroom doors. Gavin pointed across the hall.

Faith knocked and then pushed the door open. Ariel lay with her knees drawn up, crying. Gretchen stood by her, pale as she could be. Faith asked, "What's wrong, Ariel?"

"Cramps...sharp, painful cramps," Ariel replied.

Nanny was there by that time. "Where does you hurt, child?" she said softly. Ariel pointed to her stomach. Seeing Gretchen, Nanny spoke to her, "Go get Mrs. Martha. The rest of you mens get out." She stood up and whispered to Faith, "Get some towels and some more sheets, Honey. I think yo friend is about to lose her baby."

They stayed at Live Oak for another week. When they got back to Gavin and Carolyn's house, Gabe sent Hex to get Captain Davy. "You can tell him that Ariel is fine, but she's lost her baby and needs him."

It was late the next day by the time Hex and David Davy returned. Gabe broke the news to him on the porch of the Lacy's house. "She's afraid that you will be disappointed in her," Gabe said. "You have got to convince her that you are not disappointed."

Davy went to Ariel and they walked to the room that she was sleeping in. Ariel immediately started crying. "I've lost our child."

"Shhh...," Davy said. He sat on the bed and pulled her to him. "The only thing I care about, dear wife is you, and that you are well. You are the most important person to me. If we have children, good. But if not, that's alright. You are the most important thing on this earth to me," he repeated. "You are what makes my life worth living and don't you forget that. You, Ariel Davy."

Davy lay back on the bed and pulled his wife to him. At some point peaceful sleep overtook them. When they awoke the next morning, Ariel laughed. "You didn't even take off your boots."

PART II

An Ole Salt

I'm writing you this letter
There's things I gotta say
The innocent boy that sailed away
Returns a man today

It were a mighty warship
On her rolls I signed my name
After thirty years at sea
Its salt water that fills me veins

They tell me I must retire
My able days be done
And what the sea took away
The sea now returns

Michael Aye

CHAPTER TWELVE

"SIGNAL FROM *THALIS*, SAIL to larboard," the lookout called down.

The island of Antigua was expected to be sighted before sundown, per the master's prediction, so Gabe was not surprised to hear the call. HMS *Thalis*, in keeping with sailing orders, was in the lead of the squadron. With merchant ships in large convoys headed to the Indian Ocean and small coastal traders plying the Caribbean, Gabe had been surprised that they'd not spotted more ships. It was four bells in the afternoon watch or, as No had explained to Gretchen, it was two o'clock. Gabe could see a bit of haze off in the distance, making him wonder if that was Antigua.

Faith and Ariel were off to starboard, passing the time of day. Faith had confided to Gabe that Ariel was concerned over her inability to carry a child. She wanted to give David a son, so badly. She had told Faith that she was worried, having been abused as a child sex slave, that it may somehow, have prevented her from being able to have a child. Dagan had rescued the girl, freeing her from that awful existence. She'd fallen in love with Davy but had been worried, wondering if she could enjoy a man after her ordeal. Dagan had said that love would find a way, and it had.

The new doctor walked out on deck. Doctor Honeycutt had done a good job with Captain Skidmore. After a report had been sent to Bermuda, Gabe had thought that the commander there might have sent a dispatch vessel to bring the young captain home. Gabe decided to bring the captain along with them, after hearing no word from Bermuda. At some point, he'd probably send Troy back to England. Doctor Honeycutt now had Troy up and exercising under the watchful eye of his cox'n, Peter Finch. The idea of having another doctor, other than Robert Cornish, had taken a bit of getting used to. Thinking about the doctors brought Doctor Cook to mind. He and Jimena had decided to stay in Savannah. Starting a new practice should be easy with the number of people there living there.

Gabe had invited Honeycutt to dine with him a few times, along with some other officers. He'd seemed very affable and got along well with the officers in the wardroom. Hex related that the crew liked the good doctor. Hex had also said that he was quick to pick up on those who were not sick or injured. The lame and lazy element of the ship found out quickly that they'd not get over with Doctor Honeycutt.

The lookout called down, breaking Gabe's train of thought, "From *Thalis* captain, land ho!" Gabe looked up at the sky, before sundown the master had said, well he was right.

Captain Davy walked over and said, "Like all of his kind, old Ben Pittman knows his business."

Gabe smiled, "Did you doubt him?"

"Never, not once, I know better," Davy said with a smile.

Gabe laughed...yes, the old master from Drakkar had taught them that lesson. Old Mr. Peckham had brought his young gentlemen along well. His soft voice and firm hand had watched more than one young sir climb the lofty ladder to the quarterdeck.

***

A KEY TO THE British naval forces in the Caribbean, English Harbor provided a haven where warships refitted, avoiding the long haul back to England. This was where Gabe had become a man. The island where he'd made lieutenant. There were so many memories for both him and David Davy.

Fort Berkeley jutted out on a spit of land defending the harbor entrance. High on Shirley Heights there stood another fort. This fort also had a signal station at the lookout. Gabe could see the flags being raised. They were no doubt sending a message to Fort George on Monk's Hill, letting them know that a British naval squadron was entering the anchorage. The sea seemed smooth, as if inviting Gabe's command to enter the narrow cut leading into English Harbor. The anchorage was empty except for one frigate, but it was a reminder of all the ships that were now gone. Ships under the command of men like Rodney and Hood and Gabe's brother, Lord Gilbert Anthony.

The harbor was a haven, a safe place from the elements and the enemy. A place where ships could be repaired and crews could rest. The ships were firing the salute as Gabe went down to change. He'd call on the governor while Davy spoke with the captain of the frigate.

England, now that America had been lost, had also lost a number of her West Indian colonies. Therefore, it was very important that Antigua, and English Harbor in particular, be ready to defend itself and maintain a place to refit England's ships of war.

***

THE GOVERNOR GAVE A warm welcome to Gabe and Faith. He had seemed a bit disappointed when they had not brought the new governor. Gabe explained how he had brought out prisoners of war from England to be swapped for British prisoners of war. He also was sure that a new governor would not have wanted to make the roundabout voyage they'd taken.

After visiting with the governor, Gabe and Faith found that both of the old houses they'd lived in were taken. Deborah's house up on the hill overlooking English Harbor would do for a temporary place but it was little more than a cottage. Hex whistled up a carriage to take them up to the cottage where the housekeeper, who'd been left in charge of the cottage, greeted them warmly.

"I wondered if anyone would be coming when I saw all those ships coming in," she said. Hex took the carriage back to get Gretchen, Lum, Nanny, and little James. "We'll make do 'til you get a place," the woman, Siba, said. She then mentioned a couple of people that Gabe might see who had some of the larger places in and around English Harbor.

It was crowded the first night in the cottage, but they managed. The next morning, Gabe and Hex went to the ship early. Josh provided a quick breakfast for the two, and then Captain Davy reported. He stated that the frigate was under the temporary command of the first lieutenant, a man named Bantam. The captain was over at the hospital having his leg operated on after a fall in rough seas. He'd broken his leg with the bone sticking out of the tissue.

"Damn, what a bad injury," Gabe said.

"Aye," Davy agreed, "especially when the ship's surgeon is a butcher at best. The carpenter set the fracture and splinted it, and the surgeon was dismissed from the ship when they made it to Antigua. The lieutenant reported that they'd come on debris from a smaller ship, *Sparrow*." The *Sparrow* had been a dispatch and mail vessel of eight guns. "I asked how they identified the vessel and the lieutenant showed me part of the transom that they fished out of the sea."

"This is starting to be a problem," Gabe said.

"Aye," Davy replied.

Gabe looked at his watch and said, "It's time I meet with Faith so that we can find suitable quarters."

"Major LoGiudice and Holly just went ashore, and Ariel is with them," Davy said.

"Wish us all luck," Gabe said as he and Hex made their way on shore to the waiting carriage.

Faith was accompanied by Gretchen. Nanny, and Lum had kept James. "I was told of a couple of places by Siba," Faith said as they drove off.

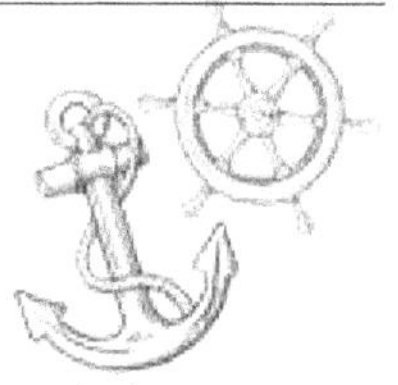

CHAPTER THIRTEEN

MR. JOSEPH MOORER, CALLED Joe, and his wife, Cecilia, met Gabe and Faith. They were both middle aged Americans who had come to the island some years ago. It didn't take long to find out they knew Deborah, Gil's wife. Now that the Moorers' children were grown up and gone, their house was more than they needed. Even though Gabe had intended to rent a house, knowing you could never tell when orders would change, the Moorers wanted to sell, rather than rent, and use the profit to buy or build a cottage.

After looking the house over, Faith was in love with it and was sold on it. It had jalousie windows that would open to let air in but keep out the rain. It was well shaded also. A closed-in well was right out the kitchen door, plus the servant's quarters consisting of two large rooms were off the kitchen as well. There was a large drawing room, a small room that could be used as a bonus room, an office, or even a bedroom. It shared the same fireplace as the drawing room. Across the hall was the dining room. You could enter it from the kitchen or from the hall. The kitchen fit behind the bonus room and the dining room. In front of the dining room was a library, the shelves lined with books. A large desk was in the room also. It was made of hardy English oak. As they entered, Faith stated that at the front end of the room, a crib could be placed for James to take naps when they were all downstairs. Gabe noticed that as Faith said this, she was rubbing the lower part of her stomach. It was something that she'd done all through her pregnancy with James. Hmm, he thought.

There was a large master bedroom upstairs that took up the back part of the house. A bathroom was in back, with only one door that entered from the bedroom. Another room that could be used as a bedroom or sewing room was to the side of that, and across the hall were two more bedrooms. A large porch wrapped around three sides of the house. There was a large stoop at the back kitchen entrance. In the back was a small stable. One side was made to park a carriage under. The center of the stable was a feed and tack room and the right side was fit for a milk cow and two horses with a small paddock. A carriage was there as well.

Joe and Gabe agreed on a price for the house. It took a sizeable chunk out of the money that Gabe had brought with him. Cecilia threw in the milk cow, seeing or believing that Faith was pregnant, or perhaps because of James. Joe told Gabe if he could repair the carriage, to consider it his.

Joe surprised Gabe then by saying, "The little cottage across the street is for sale. It is smaller than what we want, but for just a couple it would do well."

Faith looked at Gabe, "It would be perfect for David and Ariel."

"I'll speak to my captain," Gabe promised. "It would be just right for him and his wife."

"I will consider it under contract until you say otherwise," Joe said.

Gabe and Faith were getting ready to depart when Joe and Cecilia invited them to their plantation for a few days. "Once we get settled, we'll take you up on that offer," Gabe promised.

The next few days flew by. The carpenter, Joseph

Morales, and two of his mates were kept busy by Faith. One of Morales' men was good with leather, and with Hex helping, they restored the carriage. Captain Davy and Ariel bought the small cottage across the street. When the carpenters finished up, Faith had their household goods sent from the ship. Cecilia Moorer had the milk cow brought over and Gabe bought two horses.

***

TWO SHIPS THAT HAD been sent out on patrol quickly returned with grave information. HMS *Thalis* 36 and HMS *Venus* 32 had met with a dispatch vessel from Tobago. They had stopped overnight on Barbados and sailed southerly the next day. A day out of Barbados, they came upon the mail packet carrying the news of Tobago being attacked. The attack had been carried out by two ships flying no colors, but one had been a Spanish frigate. The other ship was large but not like one that anyone had ever seen the likes of.

"Damme, but what's going on," Gabe said. "The war is over, and Spain signed the agreement like everyone else."

"We sailed back as there was no sense continuing, since there wasn't anything that we could do," Captain Bahnsen explained. "I did tell the captain of the postal packet to stop here on his return to England," he said.

"Good, I need to send a letter to the Admiralty," Gabe replied.

The entire naval anchorage seemed moody and subdued. A relentless squall drove across the area, testing the theory that English Harbor offered a protective bay from storms. The wind whipped the enclosed water into white caps. The waves were slamming into the ships at anchor. The ships strained at their cables and a whistling sound went through the riggings. Palm trees bent and moaned as the wind blew. Occasionally, dead fronds would break loose and fly about, with some of them slamming into the sides of buildings. A few people dashed about, at first, but as the force of the wind grew no one ventured out.

Gabe, Hex, and Lum ran about closing the jalousie windows. A chair banged against the wall on the front porch and then was blown into the yard. The squall left as quick as it started, lasting no more than half an hour.

Hex came up to Gabe, "I'm glad that came through before we left harbor."

"Aye," Gabe agreed with his cox'n.

Faith and Ariel were looking out the windows as Lum was opening them. "There doesn't seem to be much damage," Faith said.

"It wasn't a real storm, just a little squall," Gabe responded.

"That may be," Ariel said, "but I'm glad that Gretchen came and got me. I would have been frightened by myself."

"We wouldn't leave you alone at a time like that," Faith replied.

Ariel smiled, "I'm just glad that David bought that little house, with it being so close."

Gabe cleared his throat, getting Faith's attention. "We should be back in two weeks, I trust." Faith walked to the door with her husband.

Hex had taken their things to the ship the previous evening. The bonus room off the kitchen had been given to Jake. He could come and go through the kitchen without disturbing anyone. When Faith had mentioned an upstairs room, Jake had refused.

"But it's small, Jake," Faith said, speaking of the bonus room.

"It's not that small and compared to a ship, it's huge. I doubt that *Nimble's* captain has any more space," Jake replied. The discussion ended than.

Lum got the carriage out and drove them to the waterfront. Captain Bahnsen had sent a boat to pick them up as soon as the rain stopped. The commodore was shifting his flag to *Thalis* for the trip to Tobago. HMS *Active* with Laqua, as its new captain, would be joining them. Captain Bahnsen had watched Laqua handle the frigate and quickly understood why the commodore had put him in charge of the ship. *The man was a seaman…a damn fine seaman.*

CHAPTER FOURTEEN

CAPTAIN DAVID DAVY WATCHED as Captain Troy Skidmore walked over to the starboard rail. His cox'n, Finch, was at his side. Troy's recovery seemed to be coming along well. His physical recovery, that is. He obviously still brooded over the loss of his ship. *Hell, anyone would*, Davy thought. But what made the matter worse was his commander at Bermuda had yet to respond to the report Sir Gabe had sent. *Did the man care so little for his captains*, Davy wondered. At the least, there should be an inquiry into the loss of his ship, HMS *Ferret,* and that of HMS *Spitfire*. No blame should be attributed to Captain Skidmore, after an unprovoked attack by a much larger ship during peace time. Maybe he'd invite Troy to dine with him tonight. Thinking of inviting Troy to dine made Davy also think that he should check with Ariel. Calling for his cox'n, Davy wondered for the hundredth time, *how did a kid from Cornwall ever get a name like Fin*? He said it was from a fish, like a fish's fin. Fin Trehnock, an able man and for three years now, he had given Davy not one regret in choosing him.

"Aye, Cap'n," Fin reported.

"Take the next boat ashore and ask Ariel if she has any plans for supper tonight. If not, I intend to invite Captain Skidmore to dine."

"Aye, Cap'n. The purser is about to go over."

"Good then," Davy replied. As he watched Trehnock go, Davy saw men coming up from their messes after eating a quick dinner. It was a quick dinner because even with a wind sail to funnel fresh air, or any available breeze, down into the lower decks, it was still hot down in the mess. Davy wondered if it was as hot in Tobago. With a smile he wondered if, after they returned, Captain Bahnsen would have felt the honor of having the commodore on board was worth sleeping in the chart room.

***

THE GOVERNOR OF TOBAGO was relieved to see the British flags flying from the masts as the ships approached Bacolet Bay. He and his aide met Gabe at the waterfront. Introductions were made and Gabe soon found himself sitting under an awning next to a palm tree enjoying a ginger beer that some of the governor's slaves had made. It was a bit different than that in England, but it did have a good flavor as well as a little kick.

Governor Ricketts outlined the attack on the island, as they drank the ginger beer. He was adamant the ships were Spanish, which went along with the other report that Gabe had already heard. Ricketts went on to explain that control of the island had changed so many times between England and France that he would not been surprised if the attack had been done by the French. But Spain...why did they attack? The governor then confided that out of the island's population of over fifteen thousand people, only five hundred and forty were white, and that included women and children. Should some country excite a slave revolt, they'd all be wiped out.

After a hearty evening meal where the officers of both ships attended, the ships set sail the next morning. Between the rum punch, foul black cigars and late hours, more than a few were suffering the consequences.

HMS *Active* was in the lead on a course for Barbados. The sky had a beautiful look, blue with puffy white clouds lazily passing overheard. Gabe, standing by the stern rail, was watching as a pod of porpoises followed along.

Shouts from the lookout broke Gabe's reverie. "From *Active*, gunfire! Request permission to investigate."

"Permission granted," Bahnsen yelled to his signal midshipman. He then turned to his first lieutenant, "Let's clamp on more sails, Mr. Dell."

"Aye, Captain."

The bosun's pipe shrilled out as hands put down their chores and rushed to make more sail. As Gabe watched, Doctor Cook came to his mind. *What was it he said, "Organized chaos."* Under full sail, *Thalis* seemed to be dragging along. With no more than a gentle breeze, Bahnsen cursed. *Active* seemed to have caught more wind as she was now almost out of sight.

"Mr. Dell!"

"Aye, Captain," he replied.

"Let's see if we can get a few more knots out of her by wetting the sails," Bahnsen responded.

Gabe smiled, Bahnsen was not happy that *Active* had pulled away and was doing all in his power to catch up. In theory, wetting the sails should cause the thread to swell and thereby increase the action of the wind on them. Gabe had done it before and, according to the log, he had gained two knots. A bucket brigade was put together and the sails were doused.

"I believe we've picked up a knot or two," Dell said, getting a dubious look from Manton, the master.

A few minutes later, Gabe thought he could feel a bit of wind on his face. In a quarter of an hour, he was sure of it. The crew cheered, most of them thinking the increase in speed were due to the wetting of the sails, but the wind had freshened. Gabe caught the eye of the master. The old shellback gave a little smile. Gabe gave a slight nod in recognition.

They finally reached the approximate location of where *Active* had been when she sailed off. *Thalis* now had the same wind. The sails were taut and their speed picked up. It was still another half hour before *Active* was sighted and nearly an hour before they caught up. The sound of gunfire reached *Thalis* before that.

The lookout called down, "Looks like a convoy and *Active* is firing at the enemy."

ENEMY!!! *What damn enemy*, Gabe wondered. *Are we at war again and we've naught to know of it*. Bahnsen looked at Gabe, asking the same thing.

"Are we at war again, Sir Gabe?"

"Damned if I know, Chris," Gabe said, using Bahnsen's first name. The act didn't go unnoticed by the master and first lieutenant.

When they drew close, they could see that it was a convoy of Honest John's protected by a lone eighteen gun sloop of war. The convoy came together very quickly after Laqua joined in with Captain Larkin of the Bombay marines' ship, *Alacrity*. Captain Larkin was hell bent to protect his convoy but against two large ships, he'd have been sunk and the convoy destroyed, had not *Active* joined in.

"I fired before we were in range," Laqua told Gabe. "I put the signal, enemy in sight, and after a few shots with the bow chasers they buggered off. Of course, they'd all but sunk two ships in the convoy."

"I was told," Captain Larkin volunteered, "that my ship was to protect the convoy from any pirates. I certainly wasn't expecting Spaniards. I certainly didn't expect to see a damn xebec in these waters."

"A xebec?" Gabe repeated.

"Aye, Commodore, a damnable big one, at that.

The frigate was a thirty-six or a thirty-eight gun frigate, I'm thinking."

Laqua spoke up then, "It was certainly a Don frigate, but they were not flying any colors, Commodore."

"It doesn't sound like pirates," Larkin threw out. "They don't go out to sink a ship. There's no profit in that."

"Aye," they all agreed.

I've got another report to write, Gabe thought.

CHAPTER FIFTEEN

GABE SAT AT HIS desk in *Centaur's* great cabin. Simon Davis, also called the hanged man by the crew, sat in a chair beside him. On the left corner of the desk sat a pile of official correspondence that Davis was to sort through. A stack of papers already signed lay in a pile on a chair in front of him. There were more papers under a stack of official mail. The mail packet from Portsmouth and a dispatch vessel had both dropped anchor at English Harbor that morning. A bit of planning on someone's part could have combined the mail and dispatches into one and saved, at least, one of the two ships a trip.

Jake Hex had said, "That would have taken a billet away, in all likelihood, from some admiral or someone in Parliament's nephew."

Gabe continued to add more to Davis' stack and put an occasional envelope to the right, which was the pile the commodore tended to review personally, at least initially. Davis watched as Gabe casually tossed admiralty correspondence aside. However, he showed great interest in two letters. One of them was from Sir Gabe's brother, Vice Admiral Lord Gil Anthony. There was also a letter from Lord Skalla, which Gabe had put on top.

Gabe called Jake over and gave him a handful of letters. One was to Jake, two or three of them were to Faith, also there was one to Gretchen, and one in a flowing handwriting to Captain Troy Skidmore. No had one as well, it was from his grandfather, and a letter was addressed to Gabe and Faith together, from Gabe's mother.

"Make sure that these get where they need to go, Jake. Tell Faith to go ahead and open the ones from mother," Gabe said. As Jake was about to leave, Gabe called him back, "Here's another one for Faith from her aunt and uncle in South Carolina." Faith would have to give them the Antigua address so the mail wouldn't go to England first. "Take your stack, Simon, and go through it. You can use the table if you like." He noticed that his glass was empty and said, "See if you can round up Josh and bring us some more lime-juice."

"Aye, sir," Davis replied. He picked up his correspondence and gave a glance at Gabe and smiled. He'd made a mental bet that the commodore would open the letter from Skalla first, and he had. He was getting to know his master pretty well. However, he was quick to realize that he had never had it so good. The job as Sir Gabe's secretary had already offered him more than he'd ever believed. He also knew that Sir Gabe's status would only go up. He'd heard some time back that Gabe was the bastard son of an admiral. But that hadn't hurt him any that Davis could tell. Gabe had already been knighted when Davis went on board *Ares*. Since then he'd brought back great wealth from the Pacific. He'd made friends in high places, his mother had married an earl and now Gabe was a baronet. The only thing Davis questioned was why he continued to put his life in danger by staying in the Navy. He had mentioned that to Jake Hex once and Hex had replied, "It's the only thing that he's ever done, the same as his brother and father."

Davis, setting his armload down on the table, noticed that Gabe had taken the chair that he had been sitting in and propped his feet up in it, and was reading Lord Skalla's letter.

> Your second letter reached me before I posted the response to your first correspondence.
>
> I must say the absolute knowledge of the ships creating havoc has been beneficial. It is known that Spain has a few of the xebec frigates. For one to have been sent to the waters off Bermuda and into the Caribbean is in itself a bit unusual. However, my sources tell me that if such a ship is in your waters it would likely be the *La Cazadora*, or the *Huntress*. Her captain is said to be one of the most ruthless men in the Spanish Navy.
>
> Unlike most Spanish officers, however, he realizes that his ship is only as good as his men. Therefore, he rewards them with plunder, drink, and women. For him to be sent out to destroy shipping lines is the question at hand. Spain, of course, will deny any knowledge of his activities and say that he has become a pirate. We know who is behind his activities, but why? He must have something to show to the governors of Spanish held islands for them to keep him replenished and supplied. As to his cohorts, there's not a clue. Getting back to the why! Spain did not come out all that well for siding with France and the Colonies, or to be proper, the United States. But why attack British ships? France and the Americans are the ones who let them down. As I find out more, I will keep you informed. I may even send out an agent. A lion of a man, whom you know well. Your humble servant.

The ending, your humble servant, made Gabe laugh. Skalla's letter may have, at least, let him know who was in charge of these attacks, if not the reason. The agent described as a lion of a man could only be Leo Gallagher...Leo the lion. He'd once killed a man in front of a crowd and disappeared before anyone, including Gabe, realized a shot had been fired. Leo, the lion...yes, he was a most capable man. If anyone could sniff out the why, Leo would be the man.

Gabe was all smiles after reading the letter from Gil, his brother. A big surprise was coming. He thought of keeping it a secret, but was sure that Faith would be needed. So he would tell her that evening. Gabe completed his day's work and dismissed Simon Davis, telling the secretary that was enough for the day. He knew, however, that the man would not stop until he had everything ready for his commodore.

Gabe saw Doctor Honeycutt on deck, the doctor waved and then hurried on toward the wardroom. The bell for the last dog watch had just rung and the crew rushed about. *Was it that late already*, Gabe thought. At least Hex had gone ashore and he would have told Faith of the dispatch ship, so she knew that he'd be later than usual. Seeing his flag captain, Gabe called, "Are you going on shore?"

"Yes, if you are."

"Good, we'll just take the one boat," Gabe replied.

Captain Davy asked, while waiting on the boat crew, "Was there anything in the dispatches about Captain Skidmore?"

"No," Gabe responded.

"Damme," Davy muttered. "The man deserves more than that."

"I agree," Gabe admitted. "I shall write another letter to the Admiralty."

"He's getting fed up wasting away on board the

flagship. If he were not a captain, I'd have him standing watches," Davy said, adding, "He is eating in the wardroom. I've agreed to cover his mess bill until he can get some pay. He and Laqua have it off really well. I was thinking of speaking to Ron and see if he felt comfortable letting Troy go out with him on his next patrol."

"Damn," Gabe hissed.

Davy stopped and looked at Gabe, who smiled. "We'll need an officer's call tomorrow, David. The Admiralty has approved Laqua's swab. He's been promoted to Captain. It slipped my mind after getting two other very important letters, one from Gil and one from Lord Skalla."

Gabe filled Davy in on Skalla's letter after they'd been taken ashore. "Maybe we'll get some answers now," Davy said.

***

GABE BROKE HIS NEWS to Faith, after a rather large supper. "The island is about to get a new governor," he said, all smiles.

"I know," Faith replied. "Deborah sent a note with your mother's letter. They are coming for a visit in either August or September. We will have a full house. In addition to your mother and William, Becky and Hugh are also coming."

"Have you told Gretchen?" Gabe asked.

"Yes, and she replied that it doesn't mean she is going back, as long as she is welcome here," Faith responded.

Gabe nodded his head and thought; *I'll have to talk to Faith in private about that*. Later that night, he got out of bed and opened the window a bit more. It made the single candle's flame flicker causing shadows to dance on the wall. As he put the mosquito net back in place and wiggled beneath the sheet towards

Faith, she sat up.

"I've a surprise for you, dear husband." The cover was such that Faith's breasts were uncovered and his eyes were glued to them. Faith placed a hand under his chin and lifted his head to eye level. "That's what's got me in the way I am."

"What?" Gabe asked.

"I'm pregnant. I'm with child, Gabe."

A big smile broke out on his face, "We'll have more to celebrate tomorrow besides Ron Laqua's promotion."

Faith smiled, "Doctor Honeycutt was by today and confirmed it. You know, Gabe, after we made love in my old bed in Beaufort, I had a feeling I'd conceived. Nanny said that she already knew and says it will be a boy."

Gabe replied, "As Nanny says, praise the Lord." Faith smiled as she pulled Gabe to her and they kissed.

Damned if today wasn't full of surprises. He drew Faith to him. Snuggled close as they were, sleep soon overtook them. He'd never dreamed about James, but that night he had a dream. He dreamed that he saw Jake, his second son, on a quarterdeck. Jake? Yes, he'd name the boy after the man who'd saved his life. It never crossed Gabe's mind that the child would be anything other than a boy.

CHAPTER SIXTEEN

THE WETTING DOWN OF Captain Ronald Laqua's swab and the announcement that Gabe and Faith were going to have another child went over perfectly. It did create a lot of effort on Josh Nesbit's part, but Captain Davy sent his servant and a wardroom servant to help out. Captain Lee Honeycutt volunteered to swap patrols with Laqua so that he could see the local tailor to get new uniforms. Captain Troy Skidmore and his cox'n, Finch, were invited to go on patrol with Honeycutt and when they returned they'd go with Captain Laqua.

Doctor Honeycutt, at one point, sidled up to Gabe and promised that he'd look in on Faith at different intervals to see how she was doing. The offer for some reason touched Gabe.

"Thank you, Hunter," Gabe replied. "Your offer is most welcome." Those standing close by did not miss the commodore using Honeycutt's first name.

"I've delivered one hundred and five babies thus far," Honeycutt said. "It seems that I'm always about when a mother's time comes."

Captain Troy Skidmore had watched the proceedings somewhat in awe. It was very obvious that this was a happy band of officers. When he'd eaten with Captain Davy and Ariel, he was quick to realize that the commodore held a special place in the captain's heart. He also heard interesting things about his Uncle Dagan. Dagan, he'd met but only briefly. The big surprise to Troy came when, after announcing his wife was with child, Sir Gabe had called his cox'n forward and announced that if the child was a boy, and he had Nanny's guarantee that it was, and this brought laughter from everyone. If the child was a boy, he'd be named Jacob, Jake for short, after his best friend and cox'n, Jake Hex. The captains gave another round of applause when the commodore and Hex shook hands. There were lots of captains who showed favor to their cox'n, but Troy had never heard of a son being named after one.

***

THE WIND WAS A moderate breeze coming from the east, nor-east. The sky was clear and the sun shone down brightly. It was a good day to be at sea. Turks and Caicos lay to the northwest, and then there was the Bahamas. The Bahamas was the northern most aspect of HMS *Venus* of thirty-two guns patrol area. The Crooked Islands northward were under the Bermuda squadron's responsibility.

Troy mentioned this to Captain Honeycutt, "I wonder how much patrolling gets done with them down two frigates." He then told Honeycutt about the friction and unrest between Bermuda and Turks and Caicos. "It is mostly over the salt taxes. Therefore, Turks and Caicos have received little attention from the Navy." Honeycutt thought this odd, but knew a lot of the islands were very independent.

They spied a coastal trader as *Venus* come about and headed back southward. The captain of the trader was a jolly older man with a belly so rotund, it stretched at the buttons on his shirt. He related that he was headed to San Juan. Honeycutt asked the man if he had any Cuban cigars.

"Si," the man answered. He spoke rapidly to a mate who went below and came back up with three boxes, swearing the flavor was smooth and had little unpleasantness.

Honeycutt smiled, he'd not heard a cigar described that way. After paying the trader in gold, the man opened up. His fear of being boarded and his cargo taken was relieved; he offered a sample of some very fine wine. Honeycutt and Troy went down the entry port to the little tender. The wine was good; more of a sweet dessert wine, but Honeycutt bought a case.

The captain then spoke of the two Spanish warships that he'd spied leaving Cuba. The ships passed so close to his little lugger that he worried it would broach. One of the ships' men threw a bucket of slop on his little ship and laughed about it. Honeycutt showed sympathy for the captain's ordeal.

The name of the lugger was *Elena*, after the captain's daughter. The little captain said that his name was Pepe. Honeycutt promised to tell his fellow captains to keep a lookout for the *Elena* and if she was in trouble they would help as they could.

Honeycutt thought to himself as they were sailing away, *he had one more piece of the puzzle as to the two Dons.*

***

THE MAYOR OF SAN Juan had had his fill of complaints in regards to the ships, now setting under the fort's protective guns. He had waited an hour already to see the captaincy general. San Juan had dealt with the sailors from Spanish warships many times. But neither Capitán de Fragata Juan Alvarado nor Mateo Monterio seemed the least bit concerned when he, Angel Santiago, mayor of San Juan came to the men to complain of how their crews treated all the women, as if they were *putas*.

When a man stood up for his wife or daughter, several of the crew would jump him and beat him severely. When damages to a cantina or tavern were asked for, the owner was laughed at. The captaincy general had put off seeing San Juan's mayor, because he knew that at best, there was very little that he could do.

The Capitán de Fragata had the backing of Spain. Should he, the captaincy general, demand that the sailors act as they should, he would get little, if any, backing from Spain, and might even find himself recalled. That was not something that he wanted. He lived well as the captaincy general in San Juan. In Spain, he'd be just another former government official, not much better than a peon. Why didn't the ships leave and go do their devilish deeds and then rest at some other islands?

Instead of inviting the mayor into his office, he walked out to the waiting area, "Come, let us go see these capitáns together."

A carriage was brought around and they were taken to the waterfront. The ships were gone. They had sailed away that morning. A sense of relief came over both men. Hopefully, they'd be gone for a while.

***

THE *ELENA* ANCHORED AND Pepe came ashore in time to see the official coach leaving the waterfront. When he got home, his wife was hysterical. Her niece, Consuelo, and another girl had been taken by the ships that left that morning. The whole area had been searched. They'd last been seen in the company of Capitán Alvarado and the other capitán. That had been yesterday. Consuelo was just sixteen and Marianna was only seventeen.

"Oh, why did they take these young girls," his wife cried.

Pepe knew why, and he also knew that it was too late to do anything to save the girls. They'd both be used up by the time any rescue could take place. But without knowing where the ships were going, how could any rescue be attempted? Pepe also knew when the capitán grew tired of the girls; they'd be turned over to the crew or thrown overboard for the sharks. It came to Pepe then, instead of resting at home a week, he'd sail again tomorrow. He'd skip his usual stops and sail to Antigua. He'd alert the British about the ships and the girls. Tonight, though, he'd go down to the waterfront and find out all he could on these sons of Satan.

The *Elena* sailed into English Harbor with a white flag flying at the mast. Pepe knew that none of the warships would be concerned with his little trader. He anchored and was rowed over to the largest ship, knowing it would be where the commander of these forces would be. He was soon allowed to board and only waited a few minutes before the flag captain arrived. After telling Captain Davy about his situation, Pepe was escorted to the commodore's cabin.

Sir Gabe welcomed the little man and provided refreshments. They were soon in earnest conversation about the rogue Spanish captains. Pepe explained that it was only out of fear that they were allowed in San Juan. He wept when he told how the girls had been abducted. He then gave Gabe all the information that he'd obtained on the captains.

Gabe was touched with the plight of the people of San Juan, and Pepe's family in particular. He then pledged the support of the Royal Navy. Pepe left the ship feeling much better. Gabe had been blessed with a box of Cuban cigars.

***

The full moon shone bright, its reflection only broken by a gentle sea. Even without the lanterns, the deck was light enough for the crew to see. HMS *Centaur* pushed through the gentle swells so that very little motion was felt by the crew. Directly astern to *Centaur* sailed HMS *Active* to larboard, and to starboard, HMS *Venus* held her position.

Captain Bahnsen's thirty-six gun frigate, *Thalis*, and *Nimble*, the fourteen gun sloop of war stayed back and watched over English Harbor.

On the deck of HMS *Centaur*, the commodore's cox'n had the men mesmerized with the song he was singing. Even the captain and the commodore stood by the fife rail, as taken in by the cox'n's talents as anyone.

For three thousand miles or more
I sailed across the sea
To the island of Grand Cayman
Where a lovely girl waits for me

I remember the song they sang
As she danced so close to me
And I recall the angry stare
From her father that I received

To marry a common sailor, was not the
Marriage that he had planned
To give her the life she lived
Would require a wealthy man

I sailed away distraught
Over the words he had said
But I vowed that I'd find a way
So that we could be wed

I heard a story long ago
It told about the pirate, Captain Kidd
In a cave far away
Lay a treasure he had hid

The mystery of the treasure
Told by an old man
His father's father sailed with Kidd
And he knew the place to land

Now we're sailing back, my ship is sitting low
Such a treasure in her hold
Her father will change his mind
When he sees all my gold

As we let go the anchor
I see my Maryanne
Her love never wavered
Now she rushes to her man

For three thousand miles or more
I sailed across the sea
And I married that lovely girl
Who had waited there for me.

When the last verse was sung, the men just sat there for a moment, and then they began to clap and cheer.

"I've never heard that one," Captain Davy said. "A bit long but good, and the crew loved it."

"I think it's a bit about Con Vallin's girl and possibly his mind was on the girl he'd met," Gabe said.

Davy shook his head, "A sad story, that one."

"Aye," Gabe responded. "Hex has had his women but none really touched his heart, like she did."

Davy smiled, "I saw Joe Moorer's daughter watching him not long ago."

"Aye, she's been a friend to Gretchen, but she's too young for Jake," Gabe said. "Let's have a drink before we retire, David."

Smiling, David Davy replied, "You talked me into it."

Josh Nesbit had been on deck listening to the music and songs. He had, however, kept his eye on the commodore. When he headed to his cabin, Josh followed. As he entered the cabin, he asked, "A brandy?"

"Aye, Josh, a good one." As the brandy was being poured, Gabe stepped to his desk and brought a paper back to the table. He had listed the places the little Spanish trader had told him were known harbors for the Spanish raiders.

The places given were Santiago, Cuba, San Juan, Caracas, and Maracaibo, with the last two in Venezuela. "There must be another," Gabe said. Looking at the map laid out before them, Gabe traced the Gulf Coast of Florida. Taking a sip of his brandy, he appeared deep in thought. "Pensacola," he said. "Tomorrow we will change course for Pensacola."

"Aye," Davy agreed. "We can sail close to get an idea if they are in either Pensacola Bay or East Bay. With us supposedly being at peace, we shouldn't have to worry about the fort," he said.

`Fort San Carlos de Barrancas sat about six miles south of the port. Santa Rosa Island with its long sandy beach divided the sea from Pensacola Bay and East Bay from the Gulf of Mexico. Further up from Pensacola was Escambia Bay. The fort sat on a bluff overlooking the entrance to Pensacola Bay. To date no navy had dared enter the bay without being at peace.

Pepe, the little trader, had told how the ships' crews had worn out their welcome in San Juan. Could this be so in other ports? Dared the ships' captains not think that, regardless of any official documents, people would not stand to be treated cruelly but so long. They would then strike back. Not unlike Antigua being a long way from England, it was a long way to Spain from any of the ports the ships chose to use. It would be years, if ever, before word reached Spain about the sons of Satan's deeds.

CHAPTER SEVENTEEN

THE BAYS AT PENSACOLA were full of ships but there was not one warship. Honeycutt had learned, from Pepe, the names of the ships, *La Cazadora* and *La Tigresa*...The *Huntress* and the *Tigress*. They had taken their villainous crews elsewhere as they were not in Pensacola.

Sailing southerly, Gabe's squadron sailed through the Yucatan Channel and eastward to Grand Cayman. It was not surprising to Gabe that HMS *Ares* lay at anchor off George Town. It was not long after *Centaur* anchored that David asked, "Do we require Captain Vallin to repair on board?"

Laughing, Gabe answered, "I think we'd have a wait. I'm sure that he is on shore."

"Aye," David responded.

"Did you notice any other warships about, David?" Gabe asked.

"No, were you expecting someone?" David replied.

"I thought Captain Leonard Montgomery might be here with his ship, HMS *Lynx*," Gabe said.

Hex was soon back, in the cabin, with a smile on his face. "A boat has just shoved off from shore, Sir Gabe."

'I assume you know who is in it from your smile?" Gabe said.

"Aye, its Con Vallin with his woman," Hex replied.

Pelicans splashed down, creating a ten minute interval where the heat was ignored and the crew watched the ungainly birds feeding. Gulls hovered about the ship looking for a morsel of food that the sailors would throw their way. Near the shore, frigate birds could be seen at the edge of the beach eating a washed up jellyfish.

No watched the black colored bird and remarked to Pittman, the master. "I read where those frigate birds could soar for weeks on end without landing."

"Aye, young sir. I calls 'em robber birds as they steals most of their food from other birds," Pittman remarked. Laughter drifted through the skylight. "Captain Vallin has himself a pretty lady."

"Aye," No agreed. "She must care for him, having waited so long."

Down in the great cabin, Gabe, along with one or two guests, was being invited to Con and Hannah Bodden's wedding the next day. It was to take place at Pedro Saint James. Gabe had been there on a previous visit to the island. He had attended Hannah's twenty-first birthday celebration there. It was the home of William Eden, the island's chief resident. The chief resident was in fact, not unlike that of the acting governor.

Gabe had found out, during his conversation with Con, that Bermuda's commander had been recalled to England. That was reason enough for the man not to have acted on Gabe's report about Troy. Gabe also found out that Captain Leonard Montgomery had retired from the Navy at the end of the hostilities. Like many others he knew, Montgomery would probably have ended up on the beach, so Montgomery had taken the opportunity to become master of a merchant ship, with Eden's influence, no doubt.

Vallin was now the senior naval authority for Grand Cayman. However, he still had to maintain patrols over a certain area, so being filled in about the two Dons wreaking havoc was information that he needed. Thus, Vallin told Gabe of the two ships that he'd seen entering the anchorage at Roatan.

***

THE WEDDING HAD BEEN as formal an affair as Gabe had ever witnessed in the islands. Con Vallin had surprised Gabe by asking him to be his best man at the wedding. It was an honor that Gabe was happy to agree to.

The ships were back at sea now on a course for Antigua. They had not met up with the Spanish ships but most of the ports that they could use had been looked into with the exception of San Juan. Gabe had made a decision. He would center his patrols near Cuba and Puerto Rico. Sooner or later, they'd show up. He also decided to send out two frigates at a time. To not do so, meant almost a certain loss of a ship. He may even use *Centaur* with a frigate, and *Thalis* of forty-two guns with a thirty-two gun frigate, rather than sending the two thirty-twos together.

***

CAPITÁN JUAN ALVARADO CLOSED his glass. *La Cazadora* and *La Tigresa* had passed the island of Saba, and now off to port was Saint Eustatius. More importantly though, ahead and off the larboard bow was a convoy.

The masthead lookout had said four ships with a frigate escort. The convoy was moving along under easy sail. They were not from Antigua. To attack this close to one of England's strongholds would definitely cause alarm and send home a message for more help, more ships.

Alvarado had already given the order to increase sail. He took a look behind and *La Tigresa* was following suit. As in the past, they'd overtake a victim, then pour a broadside into the helpless ship. As they closed in, a flurry of signals rose up from the last ship in the convoy. The ships in the convoy all lay on more sails. Alvarado smiled and thought, *it was too late for the last ship.*

The lookout called down again from above, "Escort ship has come about." *Good*, thought Alvarado.

HMS *Warlock* of thirty-six guns had come about and was charging down the line of ships in his convoy. He intended to save the merchant ship, *Lady Lil*. *Warlock's* captain thought to himself, *Lady Lil's master would now wish he'd kept a tighter formation than he'd done*. The sound of cannons going off could now be heard.

"Enter into the log, fired on by unknown enemy." Percival Thacker was over forty and had sailed on board navy ships since he was twelve years old. In all that time, he'd never fought such a ship that was firing her bow guns. He knew that it was a xebec frigate. In the Mediterranean, they'd proven their worth. "Make an entry, one ship is a xebec frigate. The other is a large frigate."

The xebec fired again. "They hit her that time," the lookout called down.

"Have the forward guns fire when ready," Thacker called to Johns, his first lieutenant.

"Aye, Captain!"

The *Lady Lil* was doing her best to escape but was doomed if *Warlock* couldn't draw the enemy's guns away from the merchant ship.

Thacker had to shout to be heard as the bow chasers roared out. "Signal *Lady Lil* to come hard to starboard, and then be ready to fire our starboard broadside when she makes her turn. I want every gun to fire as they bear."

"Aye, aye, Captain."

The signals midshipman ran up the signals. It took longer than Thacker had expected for the merchant ship to maneuver. When she did, Thacker called to his master, "Now, damn it, now!"

As *Warlock* turned she was hit by balls from *La Cazadora*. Riggings came down and a cannon was hit, leaping in the air. The gun had just been fired, thankfully. One after another of *Warlock's* guns thundered forth. When the forward gunner couldn't fire on the first ship, he fired on the next one, *La Tigresa*. The lieutenant was yelling to keep firing.

On deck, *La Cazadora* and *La Tigresa's* metal was hammering the once beautiful *Warlock*. A cheer went up as the two attacking ships suddenly disengaged and hauled their wind. Why? *Warlock* was a beaten ship. Thacker knew this, even if the rest of the crew didn't.

Lieutenant Johns yelled, "We did it, Captain, we did it."

Captain Thacker smiled, "You'll have to get us to Antigua, Paul."

The lieutenant looked at his captain. A foot-long splinter was protruding from the captain's stomach. "Call the surgeon," Johns shouted.

Thacker held up his hands. "It's no use, Paul, I'm done for." He took a pipe from his pocket and, handing it to the lieutenant, he said, "I always enjoyed it. Maybe you will as well." The captain closed his eyes and died.

The warrants on *Warlock* were experienced, seasoned men. They went about assessing their ship's damage. "Everything is between wind and water," the carpenter reported. "The foremast is leaning, and the rails on deck are a shambles and two guns were overturned."

They had sixteen dead including the captain. Twice

that many were injured. Lieutenant Johns called to the master, "Lay a course for Antigua." He looked about and saw the *Lady Lil* sailing toward the convoy.

On board *La Cazadora*, the two bow guns were overturned and her bowsprit was shot away. But the reason they'd broken off the action was that the anchor had torn loose. A lucky shot had parted the lines from where the anchor was catted, letting the anchor fall, causing the ship to slew around. Capitán Mateo Monterio, thinking something bad had happened to his sister ship, broke off the action. Both ships had received damage to the rails and planking. The sails had been holed. Neither one of them had expected the viciousness of the attack from the British ship but both had learned a lesson. They were now on to Santiago for repairs.

CHAPTER EIGHTEEN

FROM *VENUS*, 'SHIPS AT anchor in harbor.' HMS *Venus* was the lead ship in the squadron. She would be at anchor by the time HMS *Centaur* passed Fort Berkeley. Gabe watched old Ben Pittman instructing the helmsman. "Once clear of Berkeley Point, lads, you will steer to the northwest, taking a course of three hundred-twenty degrees." Gabe had to smile. The old master was doing his best to educate his men, any one of whom may end up a master one day.

Thinking on the lookout's report, Gabe felt, at least one of those ships belonged to Lord Stanhope. So when Gabe got home, he'd see his mother and Lord Stanhope. A thought came to him and he smiled, *had Dagan been on board, he would know. Dagan always knew*. It would not be long now, however. The ship was changing course.

Hex smiled, "We're making the change just as Pittman said."

Gabe smiled. He and Hex, and many more of the men in his squadron had made the entrance more times than they could count.

The lookout called down, "Thar be a frigate at anchor." He then added, "Looks like she's been in battle, sir." This got both Gabe and Captain Davy's attention. "Her yards be a cockbill."

"Damnation," Gabe hissed. "Hex, call out my boat crew. Captain, have your signalman signal 'standby to receive commodore."

"Aye, should I go with you?" Davy asked.

"If you like, but don't let me keep you from your duties." Gabe said this with a wink, letting Davy know his duties at home, as well.

The newly promoted First Lieutenant Danforth smiled, he'd overheard the conversation. He was equally sure his name was about to be called.

"Mr. Danforth!"

"Aye, Captain." Danforth smiled, he knew it.

***

LIEUTENANT PAUL JOHNS SAT in the captain's great cabin. He'd just outlined the battle and spoke of his captain's remarkable tactics. Gabe had to agree. To turn one's ship broadside to two attacking ships had merit. He had, in effect, at least for the moment, pitted eighteen of *Warlock's* to four bow chasers of the enemy. By doing so, he'd given the convoy time to put distance between themselves and the enemy. He would not have been able to hold the position long, but it gave the enemy a battle and not a cakewalk.

After crossing in front of the frigates, the lieutenant could only look at the results. It had worked. The enemy had broken off and the convoy was saved. There was no denying the results. Lieutenant Johns had also given Gabe dispatches that were sent from the Admiralty. Thankfully, they'd not been cast overboard at the start of the battle.

The dispatches were little more than letters. HMS *Warlock* had been sent to join the squadron. Thacker, her captain, had been a man of great experience. Also, adding Thacker to Gabe's command would give him the requisite number of captains to hold a court martial for Captain Troy Skidmore. The results of said court martial should be forwarded to the Admiralty as soon as possible. The third letter was forwarded by the Admiralty but was from the Foreign Office, which Gabe knew had come from the secret section. It basically said that an agent was *en route* to further investigate the matter at hand. Had Gabe not known what the 'matter at hand' was, the letter would have meant nothing.

Gabe stood and said, "You've done well, Lieutenant. I will see Admiral Gardner at the dockyard, and see if we can have *Warlock* shipshape before you know it."

"Thank you, Sir Gabe. *Warlock* is a fine ship," the lieutenant replied. Gabe smiled, he'd never heard a man speak ill of his ship after they'd just survived a battle.

Back on the beach, Gabe spoke to Hex, "Send the men back to the ship. If I'm not mistaken that's our carriage sitting on the waterfront near where our ship is anchored."

"Aye, Sir Gabe, I believe you are right," Hex said.

Faith was there with James, Maria, Gabe's mother, and Lord Stanhope. *Damn*, Gabe thought, *I should have mentioned to Captain Davy to free up No as soon as possible.* After a warm greeting by all, Hex climbed up on the driver's seat with the driver as everyone climbed in the carriage. James was fussing that he wanted to sit up on top with Uncle Jake, so Gabe got out and lifted his son up to Jake's waiting arms.

Maria said, "As beautiful as the day is, I'm not surprised that James wants to be outside."

Polite conversation took place while they rode to their residence. Once there, Gabe was surprised again. His brother, Gil, was there with Deborah and Macayla. Macayla was now eight years old and was at the prim and proper stage, but seeing Uncle Gabe, she ran to him. With Becky and Hugh there also, it was a family reunion of sorts. Gabe was suddenly glad that they'd taken the large house, even though Gil and

Deborah wouldn't be there long.

Gabe turned around as he heard the barking of a dog. His mother had brought Sam with them. Knowing that they were coming soon and their ship being very crowded, Faith had agreed to let Sam come with them. *Damn*, Gabe thought, *I was hoping that he'd got lost*. Sam came up to Gabe smelling on his hand. Gabe, without thinking, scratched the brute behind the ears. The dog had once saved Faith's life, so Gabe was compelled to put up with the dog.

"I was hoping that you'd forget about this cur," Gabe said with a smile.

Faith shouted, "Gabe Anthony," and slapped his arm, which caused Sam to turn and growl at Gabe. Everyone laughed but Gabe. "Mama's baby," Faith said, kneeling down and hugging the dog. Sam wiggled a bit and then looked at Gabe again as if saying, 'we see who counts.'

The men gathered on the porch after a bit. Gabe took out a couple of pipes, one of which was made out of corn cob, and the other one was made of cherry wood. "Andre sent these. Kawliga made them. He said that they are very good pipes once they are broken in."

As the conversation flowed, Gil mentioned that Leo Gallagher was about; when the discussion of the court martial came up, he offered, "I could head up the court martial, as I'm the senior military person here. The regulations say the captains of five ships, and with *Nimble*, you have five captains. The regulations were not specific about rank, and that's just what we'll say in the notes, captains from five ships met to convene a court martial to investigate the loss of one of His Majesty's ships. We will make sure written testimony by the captain of the Bombay Marines and that of First Lieutenant Paul Johns, as well as that of the Governor of Tobago, that the ships were Spanish built, though no colors were flown. From what I gather the two ships were large frigates and, without provocation, they fired on and destroyed two of His Majesty's twenty-eight gun frigates. Furthermore, of the two frigates, HMS *Ferret* and HMS *Spitfire*, both twenty-eight guns, that Captain Troy Skidmore and Cox'n Peter Finch were the only two survivors. Captain Skidmore was severely wounded and would have died but for the efforts of Finch."

Gabe sat there, his mouth agape, as his brother rattled off the proceedings. When his brother was finished, Gabe said, "Do we even need to call a court martial?"

"Of course," Gil said. "The proprieties must be met." He then smiled, "I have had a meeting with Lord Skalla, so we'll convene as required, then come to our own conclusions. I will tell you though, Gabe, the captain of the *Spitfire*, John Baskins, was a masters mate that I recommended for lieutenant. He passed and worked his way up the ladder to walk his own quarterdeck. So I want to see the Dons pay for their evil scheme."

"Are we sure that this has Madrid's backing?" Gabe asked.

"Skalla is," Lord Stanhope said.

Gabe was about to say that was about as official as he could expect, but the comment died on his lips. Riding double up to the house with Leo Gallagher was No.

"I caught this young gentleman adrift," Leo said smiling.

No was off the horse and dusting his britches when his grandfather hugged him. It did Gabe good to see Lord Stanhope show the boy such affection.

PART III

Men Who Sail the Sea

You laugh, you drink, you dance
You men who sail the sea
For tomorrow who's to know
What might assail upon thee

Be it gale or sword or cannon
Or a sinking ship it be
So live life heartily
You men who sail the sea

Michael Aye

CHAPTER NINETEEN

THE COURT MARTIAL OF Captain Troy Skidmore took place the following Thursday with all the prompt attention to detail and tradition the officers could muster. There was only one witness available, but the account of the battle given by HMS *Warlock's* first lieutenant and the sworn statements of the Bombay Marine captain and Tobago's governor were presented by the defense, Lieutenant Theodore Danforth, HMS *Centaur's* first lieutenant. The prosecuting officer was HMS *Thalis's* First Lieutenant Gordon Dell. Hex had heard Dell apologizing to Troy for having to be the prosecuting officer, but Hex kept it to himself.

The proceedings took most of the morning, with it mostly being specifics in regards to approximate ships position, weather, and so forth. After the midday meal, the court reconvened with Captain Skidmore and Finch adding a bit about being picked up by an American merchant ship and taken to Norfolk. There he was treated by the local doctor until such time as his care was taken over by Doctor Honeycutt.

Captain Davy raised his hand, at this time, "I will attest to the captain's severe injuries, therefore reading in-depth medical records, I feel is a waste of time."

Vice Admiral Lord Gilbert Anthony spoke, "I agree that it will have little effect in regards to the outcome of these proceedings, but one. Captain Skidmore, do you feel yourself sufficiently recovered from your ordeal and that you are physically fit to stand before this court?"

"I do, my Lord," Captain Skidmore responded.

"Let the records thus show the captain's response and a transcript of the captain's medical records be entered as an attachment with the defense's statements."

Gabe listened and thought, *the captain's physical state would be cause for an appeal had the results gone badly.*

Captain Laqua, who knew Captain Troy Skidmore better than anyone, asked the all important question. The one question that Gabe was sure Laqua knew the answer to before he asked. The question was to Peter Finch, "Cox'n, tell me, this court, during the assault on HMS *Spitfire* and HMS *Ferret* by these large frigates, which ship was destroyed first?"

"*Spitfire* was, sir," Finch responded. "She was hit hard from the first broadside."

"I see. As a seaman in his Majesty's Navy, ever since you were a boy, do you think HMS *Ferret* could have fought off the ah...attacking ships?"

"No sir, no chance in 'ell with the one, so's the two was as impossible."

There were no more questions asked, and the court recessed for fifteen minutes, making sure that they'd covered all the requirements. When they reconvened Skidmore's sword was positioned with the handle pointing towards him. It was over, and the court found that Captain Troy Skidmore had done all he could do in the face of overwhelming odds, and that the loss of his ship was due to forces that refused to identify themselves.

After the officers drifted apart, Gabe sidled up to Gil, "I'd like to assign Captain Skidmore to *Warlock*. I think that an endorsement from you would carry a bit more influence, especially since you were head of the court martial."

"I'll see to it," Gil said.

After seeing Gil over the side of the ship, Captain Davy called on Gabe. "Next Wednesday is the first Wednesday of the month. We have a lot of midshipmen ready to take the exam."

Gabe nodded and said, "Send out the signal before I send any ships out on patrol."

Davy smiled, "I'll see to it."

Gabe then said, "Walk with me a moment, David."

They walked down to Gabe's cabin, and Nesbit automatically sat down two glasses of lime juice. After a sip of the juice, Gabe got to the point. "I intend to offer the *Warlock* to Troy Skidmore. Before I do, I want to make sure you know of no reasons why I shouldn't."

"I know of no reasons and I think it's a good idea," Davy said.

Gabe nodded, "Have the good captain report to me."

"Aye, and Sir Gabe?"

"Yes, David."

"We have three mids on board *Centaur* who I've recommended to take the lieutenant's exam. This is after careful deliberation and discussion with the master and first lieutenant." Gabe nodded. "I've recommended Mr. Stanhope."

"What about the age?" Gabe asked.

"I've known younger to be passed," Davy replied. Gabe couldn't argue that. Davy continued, "Noble is old beyond his years. You know that. He runs the cockpit, and he corrected one of Pittman's calculations on watch one day and he's got more going for him than our junior lieutenants."

"What will we do if he passes?" Gabe asked.

"*Warlock* lost a lieutenant. It will mean more to him in the long haul, Sir."

"I agree," Gabe said with a sigh. "Make it so, David. Have someone that you trust prep him a bit."

David smiled and responded, "Who better than you, Sir." He held up his hand as Gabe started. "I was just joking, Sir. Also, with his grandfather here, it would be nice for him to be in on the celebration."

"He hasn't passed yet, Captain."

"If he don't I'll eat me hat and here's me word on it," David said like one of the crew.

***

THE BOARD FOR PROMOTION was held as per navy tradition, the following Wednesday, which was the first Wednesday of September. Of the six ships present, *Warlock* was the only ship that had no midshipman ready for the exam. The total number of midshipmen competing was double the lieutenant billets. There were only three available billets within the squadron and one on Rear Admiral Gardner's staff, if a person chose to take it. All the midshipmen busied themselves getting their papers in order. When Captain Davy handed Noble his papers, Noble saw where he'd recorded time spent on board Captain Markham's revenue cutter as a volunteer.

When Noble looked up, Davy said, "I may have not gotten it completely right, but it will be enough for the board, especially as I'm their flag captain."

"Aye, sir. I remember my time with Captain Markham well," Noble responded.

The examination was given on board *Centaur*. The group gathered on the quarterdeck and was told to be available either on the quarterdeck or the wardroom, which was likely the only time some would ever set foot in it, unless they were carrying a message.

One midshipman was much older that the rest.

He'd been acting as a lieutenant on board *Thalis*. He'd become a mid late, and so this had not been good when it came to compliance with the normal expectations of a midshipman. He was the first one tested, and when he came out he was sweating but had a smile on his face. Noble had noted that his name was Bruce Easy when Simon Davis had called him. He didn't look like the test had been that easy.

Noble was dozing when Simon called him. Stifling a yawn, he made a quick stop at the scuttlebutt for a sip of water. Once inside the great cabin, Gabe took the time to introduce the board, even though Noble knew each of the men. Noble thought that it would have been more beneficial for him if Con Vallin had been there. Captain Laqua was there, so that was a plus.

After being introduced, Captain Laqua spoke, "This young gentleman is known by me so I know that his affidavits are in order, so for the sake of time, I suggest we get right into the examination."

"Do you think that your time on a revenue cutter prepared you for warships?" Captain Honeycutt asked.

"Yes sir, in regards to learning the basics, larboard from starboard, basic discipline but nothing matches the experience one gains in deep water on board one of his Majesty's frigates," Noble replied.

You smooth tongue little shat, a perfect answer, Gabe thought.

Time was then spent discussing a ship in a storm. Noble discussed his experience in one and answered Bahnsen's questions about what to do on a lee shore in a blow.

Laqua then asked what had been most frightening about passing through the Straits of Magellan.

"It was the fog in the narrows," Noble responded.

He then answered the questions about ships in the fog. He was then asked about gunnery and he gave his experience of acting as assistant gunnery officer and what he did after the gunnery officer fell. He ended that question with, "As long as there's a target, it never hurts to keep firing until the word to cease fire is passed."

Captain Bahnsen then asked if he'd ever made a landing under fire. "Not much of one," Noble admitted. "We slit a few throats and that was it, but it was hell going back to the ship." He then explained what happened and how a French officer was directing his men with gunfire that was causing havoc.

"What did you do?" Bahnsen asked. Noble hesitated and Bahnsen said, "Tell us, what did you do?" Noble hesitated again, and Bahnsen said, "Come, sir, speak up."

Gabe spoke up for the first time, "If I may gentlemen, he hesitates because I told him that it was not something to talk about. Noble took a weapon from a wounded marine, climbed up on a boulder and, with balls buzzing all about him, he shot the French officer off his horse. Seeing that, the French soldiers retreated. Our men made it to the boats and back to the ship. I must say that by doing so, Noble's actions prevented two of our foreign agents from being captured and he saved countless lives."

"I see," Bahnsen said. "A regular firebrand."

There were no more questions for Noble. There were only two more midshipmen to be examined after Noble.

At noon the following day, the list of those passed and those advanced came out. Easy was promoted and went to the staff at the dockyard. With Easy going to the dockyard, one of the midshipmen went to *Thalis*, one to *Venus*, and Noble went to HMS *Warlock*.

CHAPTER TWENTY

CAPTAIN TROY SKIDMORE WAS sitting in the captain's cabin on board *Warlock*. He'd just returned from a meeting with Rear Admiral Gardner. The repairs on the ship had been carried out and tomorrow she would be given replacements for guns destroyed in the battle.

Warlock was a once in a lifetime chance. She was rated a thirty-six gun frigate, but she was more than that. She was ordered in 1778, and was finished just as the war ended in 1783. Captain Thacker, it seemed, had backing to get such a fine ship. She was one hundred forty-five feet long with a beam of thirty-eight feet. Her complement was two hundred sixty-four men. She had nearly that many men now. Although rated at thirty-six guns, she carried much more. *Who decided on the extra*, Troy wondered. Her upper deck carried twenty-six eighteen-pounder guns. The quarterdeck had two nine-pounder guns, and ten thirty-two-pounder carronades. The forecastle had two nine-pounder guns, and four thirty-two-pounder carronades. At the recommendation of Rear Admiral Gardner, two long nines were deployed in the stern. A loss of living space, yes, but the added firepower made it worthwhile. The total was forty-six guns, plus swivels.

The ship was second in firepower only to *Centaur*. A knock, and the sentry announced Finch. Thinking about his time on the flagship, Troy recalled that Sir

Gabe's cox'n came and went as he pleased. Other men had said, Laqua more specifically, that Hex had saved Gabe's life. *Hadn't Finch done the same*? It was time that he bought him a uniform. It would be nothing like Hex's uniform, but similar to Fin Trenock, Captain Davy's cox'n. Troy had also met Bart. Laqua had said that he was Vice Admiral Lord Anthony's cox'n and he had also seen captains salute the cox'n. The Anthonys obviously took care of their people. He'd do well to do the same.

Peter Finch came in and stood at attention, waiting for Troy to speak. Troy called to the cabin servant, "Bring us a beverage, please." He then spoke to Finch, "You saved my life, Finch. We are sitting where we are because of you. As from this moment on, you are free to come and go aboard the ship as you desire, except for the wardroom. Tomorrow we'll go ashore and get you some uniforms and get you out of those slops."

"Thank you, Captain," Finch said.

"Think nothing of it, Peter. My ship is your ship from now on. If at any time you want to be released from the Navy, just say so." Finch was speechless. Troy continued, "What did you want, now that I've interrupted you?"

"It 'pears we are getting Mr. Noble Pride Stanhope," Finch replied.

"I wonder if the commodore had this in mind before I was given *Warlock*." Troy thought aloud.

"I don't think so, sir. Word is the commodore didn't even know that he'd been recommended until Captain Davy told him. Do you have time for me to fill you in on what I's learned?"

"By all means," Troy said.

Two glasses later just a plate of crumbs was left from bread and cheese, and lanterns had been lit, when Finch completed his story. "It might be good, sir, in fact, Hex recommended this, to invite Lord and Lady Stanhope to tour the ship. One more thing, Cap'n, our commodore's mother is Lady Stanhope."

"Damme, Finch, you've told me more today than I'd ever find out by myself," Troy said.

Finch smiled, "It's my job, Cap'n."

Troy shook his cox'n's hand. Now they had to get Finch some uniforms and find a cabin servant. Thacker's servant had requested to be put ashore and sent back to England. *Well, first things first*, Troy thought.

***

EVERYTHING SEEMED TO BE going well, and then it wasn't. Troy had been invited to the family celebration of Midshipman Noble "No" Pride Stanhope's promotion to lieutenant, or as his grandfather, Lord Stanhope, called it...his step up. It was actually the second celebration. There had been one celebration that was attended by the squadron's officers. The commodore had attended with Rear Admiral Gardner. It was a brief ceremony with the commissions being handed out to the newly promoted lieutenants, along with each lieutenant's duty station or ship being announced. This ceremony had taken place at a waterfront pub frequented by the ships' officers, since the commodore had first been made lieutenant, which to Troy Skidmore's surprise had not been that long ago.

The Ship's Bell had its share of serving wenches, of which more than a few were of mixed blood. One of them was a quadroon who seemed to be paying Jake Hex a lot of attention. Ron Laqua had said that while the wenches didn't mind showing off a lot of cleavage, none of them were prostitutes. He did hint that Jake Hex probably had more than a platonic relationship with Zelda Townsend, the quadroon.

The second celebration had been a family affair, with both Troy and Finch being invited. Troy met Vice

Admiral Lord Gil Anthony and the infamous Bart. Troy told Lord Anthony how Captain Baskins had spoken of his Lordship and Bart so often that he felt he knew him. Lord Anthony had slapped Troy on the back and told him that they needed to dine together soon. At one point, Troy was looking for Finch and found him in a corner laughing with Bart and Jake. They seemed to have established a great relationship.

Troy found himself sitting diagonally across from Lord Stanhope, the Earl of Gladstone, Noble's grandfather, as dinner was served. He enjoyed his conversation with the gentleman. He was quick to realize two things. Stanhope doted on his grandson, the expected heir to his estate, and he was also very much in love with the beautiful woman next to him, Maria, Gabe's mother.

The commodore had risen in rank as fast as anyone that Troy could think of. It was said that he was one of the richest men in England. Therefore, it was doubtful that he'd ever need it, but if he did, there could be no greater advocate than Lord Stanhope. Also, having Hugh English as a brother-in-law didn't hurt either.

Sir Gabe sidled up to Troy at one point, and said, "You will soon find that you have a brave and energetic new officer. Doubtless, you will have checked into his history. There are two things that I'm compelled to tell you. He is brave beyond belief, he saved my life and Captain Francis Markham's, and almost died because of it. Secondly, while he is mature beyond his years, he is still a young man. He will endeavor to do his very best for you. But, while I expect no special favors, I do ask that you show a bit of patience with him. He does learn fast and to my knowledge, he doesn't make the same mistake twice. Without getting into specifics, I will say that he survived a life that was very hard until recently." Troy was moved by Sir Gabe's words and sincerity.

On the ride from the Crown and Anchor back to the ship, Finch told of No's life until just a few years ago. Troy thought to himself, *now I understand Sir Gabe's deep regard for the boy.*

Troy had found rising very hard the next morning. Rich food, superior wine, and Cuban cigars had left him with a pounding headache and a foul taste in his mouth. He'd just brushed his teeth and shaved when the first lieutenant was at the door.

He reported that in cutting out the gun ports for the stern guns, rot had been found. So the dockyard had to take out more to see how bad it was. 'Probably bad wood to start with,' Johns had said. It was near 1:00 p.m. that the carpenters finished taking out the rotten wood and replacing it with good wood. It was ironic that the lumber came from Machias, where a battle was fought after the townspeople refused to sell the British lumber to build barracks. Now Machias lumber was going into a British warship. The delivery of the cannons was delayed another day due to the repairs.

After a brief conversation, in regards to the ship's readiness, Captain Skidmore spoke to his first lieutenant about their new lieutenant. "I'm convinced that he will make a fine officer, Paul, but just remember he is young, and while I don't expect any special attention, I want him to learn from a first lieutenant with a firm but fair hand. I understand from Captain Laqua that he was the best of the lot. I was also told by the commodore that he expects no favoritism."

CHAPTER TWENTY ONE

NEWLY PROMOTED LIEUTENANT NOBLE Pride Stanhope was at the tailors being fitted for new uniforms when he looked at the time. He was to meet Gretchen at the Crown and Anchor for the midday meal. When the tailor was finished with the measurements for the uniforms, No dashed down the street to the inn.

Gretchen was already there waiting for him. He gave the girl a kiss and then sat down across from her. Gretchen looked at the boy...man she loved. *Could I be the wife of a sailor*? Obviously Faith was, Ariel was, and even Grandmother Maria had been, but did she have what it takes to be one? She remembered her mother asking Uncle Gabe when he returned from the Pacific a very rich man, if he would quit the sea. 'No,' he had replied. 'Why not,' her mother had countered. 'It's all I know,' Gabe had replied. Would No be like that? His grandfather was not young. *Would No quit the sea when he became the Earl of Gladstone*?

Gretchen stretched her hand across the table and No took it in his. "I love you dearly, Noble."

"And I you," No replied.

"Do you really, Noble?"

"Yes." He didn't add he wasn't sure that he knew what real love was. He understood that his mother loved him enough to sacrifice her body and self-esteem to feed him. He could see what Gabe and Faith went through in the name of love. He well remembered what the girl in Costa Rica gave him saying it was her way of showing her gratitude, and that had certainly been an awakening. He mentioned none of this because he wasn't really sure he understood love but he did know when he was with Gretchen he felt good...he felt alive. He wanted to please her and most of all he wanted her to be proud of him. She had seemed proud of him at his promotion dinner, but now she seemed to have found herself in a dark mood. Was there about to be a change or as Hex said wait until you hear the other boot fall?

Gretchen looked at No and said, "Mother and Father are only going to be here three more weeks. I must decide whether to stay here so we can occasionally be together when the Navy sees fit to give you time off, or go home. If I go home, I feel it will be the end of us. You don't know how hard it was sitting in London being true to you while you were off in foreign lands."

"Do you want me to tell you what I want?" No asked.

"Yes," Gretchen replied.

"I want you as close to me and as often as can be, but I recall something Dagan said to me once. He and I had just met, and he told me if I truly loved something to set it free. If the love was mutual, that thing or person would be back. So you decide. For now, at least, my chosen career is the Royal Navy. If something happens to grandfather, that may change. But Dagan was right, if it was meant to be like Gabe and Faith, it will be. I've told you how I feel, but it's your decision. As Gabe said once, it's not all champagne and claret. It is what you make it. I leave the decision to you."

Gretchen went to speak, but No stopped her. "You'll change your mind a dozen times before sailing time." He called the server over and paid for their drinks.

"You do not wish to eat, Sir?"

"Sorry no, I've lost my appetite," No said. Taking Gretchen's hand, he said, "Let's go for a walk."

There were very few words spoken, and when they got to Gabe's place the sun was going down. Lord Stanhope saw his grandson give Gretchen a little peck of a kiss before she went up the steps.

When No turned away, Stanhope called to him, "Mind if I walk with you, son?" They'd passed several houses before Stanhope spoke. "What troubles you, Noble?" Noble explained as his grandfather listened. Stanhope then said, "You have done a fine job of handling the situation, Noble. In truth, Gretchen probably doesn't know her own feelings. Before you came along, she was the belle of the ball with suitors at every turn. She gave it all up because she fell for you, son...fell hard. Now she realizes that she gave up a gay lifestyle for you. Yet she is realizing, at best, that she will have to share you with the sea. Some women can do that, but there are many more that can't. Maria did it with Lord James. Faith, who isn't even British, gave up her country just to be part of Gabe's life. I agree with Dagan's comments, in regards to if it is meant to be. But let me say this, it's better to find out now before you've gone too far and you're faced with a miserable life."

Stanhope laid his hand across his grandson's shoulder, "You don't know how often I've regretted not taking you and your mother in long ago. If I had, in all probability she'd be alive and you'd have been taken care of properly. I didn't and my soul hurts because of that. I can't change that decision, as much as I wish that I could. So I live with a deep regret. I guess what I'm saying, Noble, is to not slam the door shut on Gretchen if she decides to go home."

"Yes, sir, Grandfather." Noble Pride Stanhope, the next Earl of Gladstone, suddenly felt closer to his grandfather than to any other man in the world.

***

MONDAY FOUND HMS *WARLOCK* racing through the water under full sail and clear sky. Captain Troy Skidmore felt exhilarated. His career and life had been returned by the results of the court martial, but it was only in the last hour that he felt alive. He had taken *Warlock* out to get the feel of her, and she was a fast ship. The first lieutenant had a man casting the log to check the speed.

"Nearly thirteen knots," the man called out.

Lieutenant Johns walked up to his new captain. "I feared that the added weight may slow us down, but it's not a noticeable difference."

"She's fast alright," Troy responded, "but remember that we don't have the hold filled with supplies for a cruise."

"Aye, sir, but even with that, she'll sail faster than most."

Troy said, looking at his timepiece, "Send the men to quarters, and then we'll have a bit of gun drill."

As the crew secured from gun drill, Troy had to admit that he had a jewel of a first lieutenant. Johns had also quietly said, "Our new lieutenant is at home with the guns. He's already found out the sea lawyers and shirkers in his division. The bosun heard him telling Sikes to stop moaning, and if he was looking for sympathy, it could be found between shat and syphilis in his new dictionary. The men all laughed, but I bet that most of them have no clue what a dictionary is. They all new Sikes and he thought that he'd get a bit of light duty with the new lieutenant." Smiling Johns said, "He didn't though."

"Give the men an hour to eat and recover from gun drill and then we'll have sail drill," Troy said.

"Aye, Captain," Johns responded.

Troy called his cox'n over. "See if there's anything to eat or drink in my cabin."

"Aye, Cap'n, but if you haven't asked for it, your servant hasn't thought of it, I guarantee." Finch had been right

Troy thought to himself, *I'll damn sure fix that once we get back to English Harbor, and that was no error.*

CHAPTER TWENTY TWO

THREE WEEKS HAD GONE by since No and Gretchen had met and talked. It was obvious to all that things were not as they had been...as they should be. It was very obvious to Gretchen's mother, Becky, and Faith. Becky thought that maybe No had tried to have his way with Gretchen.

Gretchen laughed and said, "Had that happened, I'd probably be happy." She said this in both Becky and Faith's presence. Faith recalled having those same thoughts about Gabe. Gretchen continued, "No, Mother, No has been the perfect gentleman. We've told each other that we love each other and we do, but I've realized over the past two years that No and I have actually shared very little time together. Even when we were on board the ship at sea, we didn't get to spend more than an hour or two a day together. Since we've been here I don't see him every day. I don't know how you do it, Faith. You are a much better woman than I am. I don't know if I'm able to share my life with the sea. You live almost like a widow or spinster. I want to enjoy life."

Faith nodded, "I felt your way for a while, until I realized one night of love made up for all those days alone."

"I'm glad for you, Faith, but I can't live like that," Gretchen said.

Faith smiled, "Think what it would be like if he were taken from you tomorrow, or if you never had a chance to say good-bye, or I'm sorry. If that doesn't make a difference, then it would be better that you go away. No has had almost nothing but heartache in his life, so if you don't love him enough to deal with the separation, it's better you go away. He will get over you at some point. He's dealt with worse. I just hope that his mind isn't on you when he goes into battle. That's when a distraction can kill you." She had not shouted but had spoken in a loud, firm voice.

Lord Stanhope, sitting on the front porch, had heard the entire conversation. Faith suddenly rose to the top of his friends list...damned if she hadn't.

Faith found herself shaking. She looked at Becky, who gave the briefest of a nod. Excusing herself, Faith walked upstairs where Maria was putting James down for a nap. She turned to Faith, after placing James on his little bed. "I'm proud of you, Faith. You did well." Maria hugged her daughter-in-law then.

***

IT WAS THURSDAY, AND Lord Stanhope's ship and a mail packet had weighed anchor and sailed back to England. HMS *Thalis* and HMS *Active* would act as an escort to the northern most part of their patrol area. Captain Bahnsen had spoken to Captain Laqua and felt that it wouldn't hurt to sail a bit further than normal in search of their quarry. Laqua understood that it was to add another day of protection to the commodore's people.

The family had been very surprised that Gretchen had sailed with her parents. Standing at the stern of the ship, Gretchen watched as the escort ships come about to go on patrol. With them sailed her heart. She'd made a huge mistake. *Would No ever forgive me? Could I forgive myself? What if something happened to him? What if he found another love? Oh God, No, what have I done?*

Vice Admiral Lord Gil Anthony had taken over as the island's governor. Most of the old governor's staff had wanted to return to England, but not all of them. One of those that wished to remain was one of the chefs. Bart, always looking to help out a friend, made sure that Finch knew about the man. He was thinking that Captain Skidmore might take him on.

Felix Meyer spoke English, but with a German accent. He'd been the late governor's second chef, so he helped the governor's valet on occasion. "I was paid twenty-five pounds a year, plus livery, room and board."

Troy thought a minute. "What are you making now?"

"Nothing, I'm not working," Felix replied.

"Let's give it a trial for a month. At the end if you like it you stay, and if you don't I'll give you two pounds and you can go back to shore. In the meantime, Finch and my acting servant will show you around."

As the man left, Finch told him that he'd be with him shortly. Once he was alone with his captain, Finch said, "Meyer has been trying to get a job locally for a few months. It appears that our old governor thought a lot of the man as he's at least ten quid a month more than what is made for an assistant here on the island."

Troy nodded and said, "There's that or the man is a liar about what the governor paid."

"Aye, there's that," Finch said smiling.

***

SEVERAL MONTHS HAD PASSED with little word about the two enemy frigates, other than a few attacks in the Bermuda and Jamaica areas. *Nimble*, under the watchful eye of Captain Honeycutt, and *Venus* had landed the agent, Leo Gallagher. The man was very dark skinned, so unless someone paid particular attention he could pass as an islander at a glance. He had been picked up at the agreed upon time.

Warlock had sailed with *Nimble* this time, with Gabe making the trip to pick up the agent. Leo had found out little more than the little trader had told Gabe. He asked to be carried to Pensacola, since he felt that he might find out something there, so *Warlock* sailed there.

Afterwards, they sailed to Grand Cayman, where they spent the night. Gabe had just returned to the ship when a lookout called down, "Strange sail approaching." The same word had been passed on down to *Ares*, Con Vallin's ship, that was stationed at Grand Cayman.

"We'll never get to sea in time, Captain," Gabe shouted. "Use the windlass and bring the ship around for a broadside to bear."

Vallin ordered his ship to do the same, after seeing what *Warlock* was doing. A bell was ringing on land, so the shore guns were being manned.

The lookout called down, "It's that strange frigate and a Don frigate."

"Fire your eighteen pounders as soon as they bear, Captain Skidmore, with a measure of grape, I think," Gabe said.

"Aye, sir," Skidmore responded.

The two Dons were inside of a mile and closing when Gabe gave the order to fire. *Ares* fired almost as soon as *Warlock* did. The resulting smoke was blinding. The crew was ready to fire again in less than two minutes. Coughing, the men rubbed at their eyes and waited on the order to fire again.

"They're hauling their wind," the lookout called down.

"Get underway, Captain," Gabe ordered Troy.

As the ship cleared the harbor, the signals midshipman called out, "*Ares* is following, sir."

Gabe was fuming; it had taken too long to get underway. Troy could sense the commodore's frustration. "We should have cut the cable, Sir Gabe."

"Aye," was all Gabe said in response.

The lookout shouted down. "The enemy be off the starboard bow. They are still in sight, at least." An hour later, they had begun to close, but were not yet within gun range.

Hex stood next to Gabe, "We are going to get an afternoon rain."

Gabe looked at Hex and wanted to tell him to hold his tongue...but why? He was merely passing on information. Overhead dark gray clouds scudded across the sky.

"Damn," Gabe said, "is *Nimble* with us?"

"Aye, she is behind *Ares*," Hex replied.

The little ship had been anchored closer to shore than *Warlock*. Lieutenant Dasher, having been given no orders, had followed *Warlock* and *Ares*.

"Signal *Nimble* to return to George Town," Gabe said. "If we wait, Dasher may not see the signal."

The rain came in a heavy downpour that lasted about half an hour. When the rain was gone and the sky was clear they came about.

It was another half an hour later when the lookout called down, "Debris in the water straight ahead."

Gabe felt his stomach tighten. He knew what he'd find. While they chased the one frigate, the other Don had doubled back. A move that he'd made himself. It was that or one of the frigates had taken a different course at the onset. *We followed the sighting. We saw what we were expected to see. Now Nimble had paid for his mistake.*

The wreckage was scattered close together. "Survivors in the water," the lookout called down.

"Boats in the water," Troy ordered.

Gabe looked at Troy and said, "Make sure that your lookouts are watching for the enemy and not the men in the water." *Dagan, oh Dagan, how I wish that you were here*, Gabe thought.

"It's not your fault, Sir Gabe," Troy volunteered. "You went after the only enemy you saw." *Did I speak out loud, calling Dagan*, Gabe wondered.

Out of *Nimble's* crew of one hundred-twenty men, they fished eighty out of the water. Of the eighty men, twenty of them had significant injuries and might die. Dasher was the only officer still alive and he was in a bad way. A splinter was in his eye and one arm was cut badly.

Warlock's surgeon was a competent man. His team worked quickly with the help of *Ares'* surgeon. But by the time the sun was going down, they'd lost two more men.

"Damnation," Gabe hissed.

"What cutthroats they are to fire on such a small ship," Captain Skidmore remarked. He was pale, remembering his own ordeal.

Gabe was quick to understand his captain's feelings. He was living the hell all over again. Gabe saw No standing on the quarterdeck. He has the watch, Gabe realized. He wondered if he had looked so young as a new lieutenant.

Seeing Gabe watching him, No said, "Don't worry, Sir Gabe, we'll make the bloody whoresons pay for this."

Several men heard No's comments and cheered. If the men can see such butchery and cheer over a teenager's words, then there's definitely hope in them. Hope for revenge on the Dagoes that killed their friends.

Gabe went below to see Dasher. The splinter was

gone from his eye and his arm was sewn up with a drain sticking out.

"When I saw the ship, I knew that we were done for, sir, so I had the book with documents and signals thrown over the side. There was no need to do that, though, they were out to kill us, and not take us prisoners. I think, Sir Gabe, that they were headed back to Grand Cayman but happened up on us. I had the signal, enemy in sight, run up. They fell for the ruse, I think. They cut loose with a broadside and sailed away. I'm not sure which way they headed, though."

Gabe squeezed Dasher's good hand. "Get well soon so that I can put you on another quarterdeck." *Another mistake*, Gabe thought. I should never have let *Nimble* sail alone and we left the island unprotected. It was something that he'd discuss with Troy and Vallin when they got back to George Town.

When Gabe stood up, he saw a man carrying the wings and limbs tub. *There were so many amputations... so many.*

CHAPTER TWENTY THREE

THE ATMOSPHERE AT THE captains' call was subdued. Rumors had circulated in regards to the loss of *Nimble*. This was the first official gathering, though, to explain the actual events. Gabe did not try to shirk any of the blame. He, in fact, said, "I made two tactical mistakes. I left Grand Cayman without protection and I also left *Nimble* to return to George Town on her own.

Captain Bahnsen stood and spoke, "I don't mean to disagree with you, Commodore. You saw a chance to bring the Dons to battle. Isn't that what we are supposed to do? I don't mean to question Captain Vallin's decision making. However, it was his responsibility to protect Grand Cayman...not yours."

Captain Honeycutt stood. "I agree with Chris," he said, using Bahnsen's first name. I think if I'd been Captain Vallin, I would have done the same as he did. I think my thoughts would have been what better way to protect the island than to do away with the menace. The size of the ships you were chasing is equal to, or larger, than *Warlock*. I doubt Troy's fine ship could have dispatched both ships alone. But with another ship, even the size of *Venus* or *Active*, the chances of success is much greater." A round of applause went up.

Captain Skidmore stood up, "I agree with all that's been said. I've faced the Dons so I know that we would have given a good accounting of ourselves.

Those two ships are handled by first rate captains and crews. They are not your average Dagoes. In regards to *Nimble*, I've felt the same despair as Captain Dasher. I faced the same almost certain death as Captain Dasher. If it wasn't for Peter Finch and the grace of Almighty God, I wouldn't be standing here today. I guess what I'm saying is the minute we put on the uniform; we are expected to go into harm's way. Nobody made us, we volunteered knowing we would be expected to place our ships in front of the enemies guns. Captain Dasher knew this when he gladly accepted command. Whatever is the truth behind these attacks, the fact stands, the whoresons have cast all tradition and honorable behavior aside to provoke us. To make us bring in more ships to hunt them down."

"Aye, aye, aye," went up around the cabin.

The same thoughts had occurred to Gabe. He had said as much to the Admiralty. He spoke again to the captains, "Do you gentlemen have any Spanish speaking people on board your ships? If you do, I'd like to meet with them tomorrow at midday. Let them know that the commodore will treat them to the noon meal." This got chuckles as he knew it would.

Gabe wrote his reports for the Admiralty after his few, his very few, captains left. Taking the words of his captains to heart, Gabe didn't add his thoughts that *Nimble's* loss was due to tactical miscalculations on his part. He did request more ships and any updates that the Admiralty may have discovered. Gabe knew that he would get more information from Lord Skalla and, or Leo, if for no other reason than their open-minded approach and fact gathering.

He would have to send out two ships to rendezvous with Leo soon. He decided to send them early and have them visit each of the known lairs on their way. He would also send two more north, and check out San Juan, Cuba, and any other likely spots that they may discover. He'd send Laqua's ship on the northern patrol, as he was much more familiar with them than Honeycutt was.

***

FAITH, GABE, AND HEX were invited to dine with his brother that evening. They were now living at the Governor's residence. They had a fine supper of rack of lamb, with the cook also preparing glazed carrots, whipped sweet potatoes, lemon garlic roasted asparagus. Gabe had decided to skip the asparagus until Faith commented how good it was. They also ate very tasty and crispy bread that Deborah said was honey beer bread, and apple tarts with a glaze over them. An Italian red wine was served with the meal and afterwards a coffee laced with cream and a touch of brandy.

Gabe smiled and said, "This brings back memories of Silas."

Gil replied, "It was hard leaving him behind at home, but he was close to old friends at Deerfield."

Deerfield, the Anthonys' estate was in Kent. The estate was first bought by Gil and Gabe's great grandfather. When their great grandmother had first visited the land a herd of deer were standing in a field, so she christened the estate, 'Deerfield'.

When the women had excused themselves, Gabe told his brother about the loss of *Nimble* and his own questions about making the wrong tactical decisions.

Gil said, "I don't see that you've made any wrong decisions. Given the poor information that you had, they have all been very sound. I will endorse your recommendation for a replacement and one more frigate. If the Admiralty were to send more than that, you'd be replaced with a rear admiral."

Gabe watched Faith later that night in their bedroom, as she took off her clothes and sponged off. They'd both had a bath before going to eat at his brother's house. Watching his wife, Gabe could see the growing little belly that she had. What Nanny called a little pot belly.

He got up and walked over to Faith. Standing behind her, he took her little belly in his hands. "You are starting to show," Gabe whispered.

"Humph…I'll be fat and ugly," Faith replied.

"You'd never be ugly, my dear. There's a radiance about you," Gabe said.

She smiled and responded, "I don't feel radiant unless that's why I feel hot and my breasts feel tight and hurt."

"Has the baby moved yet?" Gabe asked.

"No, Doctor Honeycutt says it's not time yet," Faith said.

Gabe took the sponge from Faith and washed her back. Afterwards, he took her gown and placed it around the post at the head of the bed. "Tonight I want to feel your body next to mine."

"You might get ideas," Faith responded.

"I already have ideas," Gabe said, and smiling he said again, "I want to feel your body next to me."

Faith looked at her husband, 'That's where it will be then, dear husband, as long as I can draw a breath."

***

Gabe and Lord Anthony's mail was ready. When either a mail packet or dispatch vessel pulled in to port, their reports and request for a replacement for *Nimble* and another frigate would make its way to the Admiralty.

Three boats tied up to *Centaur's* side at a quarter till one and three people, who each claimed to speak Spanish, reported as directed. Gabe had asked Josh to be present to check each individual's claim. The previous year, Josh had gotten very fluent speaking Spanish with the people from New Spain, or Mexico, and those from Costa Rica. Gabe's servant had volunteered for the mission, but the very fair-skinned Josh Nesbitt would never have passed as Spanish. As the men were shown into Gabe's cabin, he was surprised to see No. He knew the boy had spoken a few words of Spanish. He didn't realize that No and his tutor, Paul Dover, had spent time with Abida, Doctor Cornish's woman, and had gotten much better at speaking Spanish. After a meal of cold meats, cheese, and fresh bread with beer or lime juice, the men were evaluated. It was a master's mate off of *Active*, who was with Gabe in the Pacific last year, and No who were the obvious choices.

When Gabe was trying to decide which of the men to send, Jake said. "Send both of them, they can protect each other."

"I knew that I kept you around for some reason," Gabe said to his cox'n.

The two men were told of the selection and a plan was decided. Both of the men were given clothing such as Pepe had worn, and they were to rehearse their Spanish under the tutelage of Josh until the ships weighed anchor. They would then sail together on the same ship. The master's mate was Nemo Bay. The name amused Gabe. It was one that stood out for a sailor.

HMS *Thalis* and HMS *Venus* set sail on Monday. Lieutenant Stanhope and Master's Mate Bay sat in the wardroom of *Venus* discussing every topic that they could think of with Josh Nesbitt, making corrections on occasion. Gabe had reluctantly agreed with his servant that he could help out with the furthering of the lieutenant and the master's mate's Spanish areas of need. Simon Davis could care for the commodore's needs until Josh returned.

There was neither a dispatch vessel nor a mail packet to have in harbor to carry Gabe's dispatches. A dispatch vessel had sailed with the Stanhope ship, and that had been three weeks ago. Since then there had been no mail packet or dispatch vessel. The mail packets usually passed in crossing so Gabe was a bit worried that something may have happened to the one due. For as long as Gabe could remember, the mail packets sailed the first Wednesday of the month. During war time they were armed to fight privateers. Gabe also knew that if the packet captain was waiting on a particular wealthy passenger or rich cargo, the sailing might be put off a week. He hoped that this was the case now.

The mail packet usually sailed from Falmouth to Barbados and then up to Antigua. It was four thousand two hundred miles from Falmouth to Barbados, and took roughly twenty to forty-five days. An average trip would roughly be a month. Once they left Antigua, the mail packet would sail to Jamaica and then to North America. At some point, the mail packets might actually drop anchor every two weeks. But while a specific schedule was discussed for ships to depart Falmouth, Gabe was not aware if such a schedule had been set. However, a postal packet would be just the type of ship that the Dons would be after. Dons, yes!! He, like everyone else, was identifying the cursed ships as Dons, if for no other reason than they were Spanish built. However, he thought that there had to be significant Spanish backing.

CHAPTER TWENTY FOUR

A SHIP'S BOAT WAS PUT out from HMS *Venus* and rowed a mile to the beach at Santa Rosa Island. Two men dressed as Spaniards walked across the narrow aspect of the island to await the agent, Leo Gallagher. The two men had pistols tucked away, but in their hands were fishing poles and, making it to the bay, they cast out their lines. Some men waved from a small fishing boat and wished them good luck.

The men in the boat spoke English, so No spoke back using a combination of English and Spanish, "Gracias, Señor, luck to you."

The boat moved on down the bay, headed through the passage into the Gulf. Leo walked up behind the men. "Catching any fish?"

"No, Señor, but it's early yet." No and Nemo turned around as they spoke.

"We must go," Leo said.

The three men walked the path back to the Gulf side of the island and gave the signal. *Venus* came much closer in this time before sending a boat ashore to pick them up.

Once they were back on board *Venus*, Leo came straight to the point. "The Dons left yesterday."

Captain Honeycutt listened and then said, "It's likely they've met up with *Warlock* and *Active* then. We'll close with *Thalis* and relay your information."

HMS *Venus* closed with *Thalis* and Captain Honeycutt passed the word to Captain Bahnsen using his speaking trumpet. And then, without further word, the two ships set sail to their rendezvous at Cayo Hueso...Key West.

The small island was home to a variety of settlers, most of whom were fishermen. That was not to say an odd pirate couldn't be found there on occasion. HMS *Warlock* and HMS *Active* anchored just off the settlement. Captain Ron Laqua took a boat ashore and bought some fish and limes. The settlers grew very talkative, seeing that the British intended no harm. After *Active's* boat returned to the ship filled with limes, *Thalis* sent her boat. The gold coin for the limes loosened tongues and it was soon evident that the Dago ships had not stopped there.

It was five hundred twenty-five miles from Key West to Pensacola. HMS *Thalis* and *Venus* made the journey in four days. When they met up and heard that the enemy ships had sailed the day before *Thalis* and *Venus* got to Pensacola was frustrating. They had to have sailed to the southern aspect of Cuba while we sailed past the northern aspect of the island, the captains decided. The decision was made to sail below Cuba, past San Juan and back to Antigua. By the time the four ships anchored off English Harbor, the four captains were very disappointed. The enemy had not been sighted.

***

WHILE THERE WERE NO Baptist churches on Antigua, Faith had always attended the small Church of England in English Harbor. When Gabe was not at sea, he attended with the family. While a lot of the service seemed similar to the Catholic Church, they emphasized the significance of the Protestant aspects more than other churches. Lum summed it up saying that it was closer to the church he was raised in.

The service in the church today had many of the

squadron's officers in attendance. All the officers and crew were frustrated over not having found the renegade ships. Perhaps like their commodore, they were seeking a bit of spiritual guidance.

The overdue mail packet had not shown up, but another had. Gabe added an addendum to his report to the Admiralty. He requested that if any of the known lairs were found to be sheltering the rogues, England should consider it an act of war. He didn't know how far the Admiralty would go with such a request. Just to put it up the chain of command could take months and then Parliament would have to decide. Still, it showed the severity of the situation.

He'd also had Simon Davis make a fair copy of the letter and sent it to Lord Skalla. He had considered sending a copy to Lord Stanhope, but he knew that involving his father-in-law could come back to haunt him, so he'd not done so. Gabe had sent *Thalis* and *Active* to Jamaica as escorts for the mail packet and had recommended that the packet be given further escort by ships from the Jamaica squadron. The base commander had agreed and would escort the ship to Bermuda, hoping that they would provide the escort to Halifax. Hopefully, this packet would not be lost to the Dons.

Leo Gallagher, the agent, said that his findings in Pensacola had been similar to what they knew about in San Juan. The ships and their crews were not well-liked in Pensacola. In fact, at one waterfront tavern, one of their men was found out back with a knife stuck between his ribs. Gabe mentioned the girls that had been taken from San Juan. There had been no mention of women on board the ships that Leo had picked up on.

"Maybe we should just escort any ship or convoys that come this way," Captain Bahnsen had thrown out.

"They may have moved on to another sector," Captain Troy volunteered. "My ship was from Bermuda. Nothing says that they have to remain in our sector forever. It appears they probably decide where to go next."

"That's true," Gabe admitted. "I think that they could be anywhere between Halifax and Tobago. Another thing, they've worn out their welcome in our sector, so I feel that they've moved on. We've several islands in the Bahamas that are British possessions. They'll likely show up at any of them."

"Do they fall under your command?" Honeycutt asked.

"No, but do you think anyone will care if we take a peek?" Gabe asked.

Captain Laqua spoke then, "Let's not forget some of the islands off of Georgia and there's some along the Gulf coast of Florida where the whoresons may anchor."

"Good thinking," Gabe said. "Sanibel and Marco, I know, were used by pirates. Amelia Island on the Atlantic coast of Florida would be a good place to hide out."

***

IT HAD BEEN A month since the last mail packet had dropped anchor in English Harbor. A sigh of relief escaped Gabe when the next one arrived. Hex walked in to deliver the mail and dispatches and said, "Captain Davy is sending a ship's boat over to pick up the squadron's mail."

Gabe had intended to go on shore but decided to wait on the mail. He knew that any private mail would likely go to the post office. Faith and Lum usually enjoyed going to the post office to pick up that mail, so he decided to let Faith have her outing.

It took about forty-five minutes to get the mail sorted and a signal put up for the ships in port to send boats. Simon Davis came to the cabin with the commodore's mail.

Surprisingly, Gabe had a letter from Lord Stanhope, and concerned that something may be wrong with his mother, he tore that one open first.

Dear Gabe,

I have been in correspondence with a mutual friend who sends you his best. He wishes me to tell you that he will be seeing you soon. Your ideas caused a stir. Nobody wants to go to war right now. But neither do we want to see our ships and islands attacked. It would be good if we could by some means capture a prisoner, but I dare say that capturing a ship might be as easy. I have it on good authority that the frigate, *Storm*, and a Bermuda sloop of ten guns are heaed your way. Some thought to add more ships might mean sending a more senior man. The Prince, who got wind of this, let it be known that he felt you a most capable officer and should you decide that you needed advice, who better to turn to than your brother. How the Prince got wind of this being discussed, I must admit ignorance. I have a good suspicion but being as I have no proof, I'll not mention names. Your mother sends her best.

On the passage back to England, I watched a young lady fall into despair over returning to England and not staying there. If you should happen to have a conversation with a certain lieutenant let him know. Also, I'm sending a hundred guineas for the lieutenant to open an account locally. Let him know that his grandfather loves him and were it viable to my responsibilities, I'd live wherever he was stationed. I wish you God's speed,

Your humble servant,

William Stanhope, Earl of Gladstone

Gil had been right, Gabe thought, and if he was reading the letter correctly, then Lord Skalla would be on hand shortly. He'd probably take passage on board the frigate, *Storm*. The next letter was from the Admiralty. They agreed on the need for an extra ship and a replacement for *Nimble*. They did not name the ships nor had they said a word other than the report had been forwarded up to the First Lord.

The rest of the mail looked to be routine, so he told Hex to call out his boat crew. He then called Simon Davis in and handed him the pile to sort through, this mail they would go through tomorrow. He then fished two coins out of his pocket and handed them to Simon, "Give one to Josh and then you two have an evening on me."

"Thank you, Sir Gabe. I've work to do tonight but tomorrow we'll go on shore, I'm thinking," Simon replied.

"At your convenience then," Gabe responded. It had suddenly come to Gabe how much he'd come to rely on the hanged man. He was glad that it was one hanging that hadn't been carried out fully.

CHAPTER TWENTY FIVE

FAITH AND LUM DROVE down to the waterfront after leaving the post office. Lum stood up in the driver's seat and, shading his eyes with his hand, said, "I believe that's Sir Gabe's boat shoving off now, Missy."

"Thank you," Faith said as she continued to read a letter she'd opened at the post office. When Gabe stepped ashore, she put the letter down and called to Hex. "Jake, can you come here a moment?"

Gabe and the cox'n both walked up to the carriage. "Gabe," Faith started, "would it be alright for Jake to invite No to dinner tonight and give him this?"

Gabe smiled and said, "If he doesn't have duty, I'm sure that he'd be delighted. Either way, that letter, I think, will make his day."

Faith smiled, "Do you have plans tonight, Jake?"

"Aye, I've agreed to meet Bart," Jake replied, "but I can see No first."

"Don't get fleeced, Jake," Gabe said.

The cox'n just smiled. Bart was known to be an expert gambler. "We are not going to gamble. The owner of the Crown and Anchor wants to sell the tavern and return to England to be close to his children."

Gabe nodded, "I wonder who he'll get to run the place."

Hex smiled, "Bart has a rather...ah, intimate relation with one of the women there. Portia is of mixed birth. I'd say if part of her blood was black, she'd be an octoroon, but she's from Puerto Rico."

"If Bart trusts her, I'd say that is all that matters," Faith said.

Hex took the letter and verbal dinner invitation to No. One look at the letter and No smiled. He was not on duty that evening, so he agreed to dine with Gabe and Faith. Later, in his small cubical, called a cabin, he read the letter. When he finished he read it again. Part of him was glad that Gretchen realized her mistake. However, a part of him had seemed almost relieved when she had left. He'd never met a girl that he'd cared for like he did Gretchen. But was he ready to make a lifelong commitment? He wasn't sure. Also, she'd run off once. Would she do it again? He certainly had to think about that before he answered her letter. A part of him said she was it. He'd found the woman that he wanted to spend his life with. But!!! There was still a little something nagging at the back of his mind.

First Lieutenant Paul Johns was in the wardroom when No came from his cabin. "You going to eat at the commodore's house?" he asked.

"Yes sir, there's been letters from home and Faith asked me to come by," No replied.

"You call Lady Anthony, 'Faith?'" Johns inquired.

"Aye, she prefers it. You see, Gabe was just a young lieutenant when they met," No said.

"When we have time, I'd like to hear about our commodore. I hear that he is second to none when it comes to prize money," Johns said.

"I couldn't answer that, sir," No responded. "I will tell you, though; he is a first class fighting man. I don't believe that you would find a person alive who knows Sir Gabe that wouldn't agree to that."

"I believe you, Noble...I believe you."

***

THE MAIL PACKET LEFT the following day. HMS *Warlock* and HMS *Active* were acting as escorts. The three ships had barely cleared the harbor when HMS *Storm* and the sloop, *Thorn,* arrived. Expecting the signal, *Storm's* captain, Miles Bedford and *Thorn's* captain, Jeremy Calvert had their boats ready by the time the anchor was let go and the ship rounded up.

They reported as soon as the signal, captain repair on board, was given. Both of the men were very excited to be a part of Gabe's squadron. Basically, with so many ships laid up with the peace, they were happy to be employed. Gabe brought the two men up to date on the rogue ships when they reported.

This caused Captain Bedford to say that they had found flotsam a day ago. "There was nothing to identify the ship, but from the hatch cover and the spars she was probably a brig."

Damn, Gabe thought. He then said, "Let your needs be known to Captain Davy and we'll see that they are taken care of."

"Thank you, sir," Bedford replied.

"I have two ships out, but they should return in the next few days. When they return, I'll get you all together so that you can meet your fellow captains," Gabe said.

Captain Davy remarked, as they left, "*Thorn* looks like a Bermuda sloop."

"Aye," Gabe agreed. "She was built for our American cousins and fitted out as a privateer. She was pierced for fourteen guns but has had some modifications and now carries sixteen.

"She is ship rigged," Davy said, meaning that she had three masts. "She's like a small frigate," he said, appreciating the lines and beauty of the ship.

Gabe handed him a sheet of paper and watched in awe as Captain David Davy's expression changed.

Davy read the paper aloud, "Fourteen twelve-pounders and a thirty-two pound carronade on each side of the bow. She was completed in 1778 and rearmed in 1781. Damme, she has a greater armament than any sloop that I've ever seen or heard of."

Thorn was one hundred and ten feet long, and her beam was broad for a Bermuda sloop at thirty feet. Gabe thought that was because she was built to be a raider…a privateer. It was her beam that allowed her to carry such powerful armament for a sloop. He had noticed that she had a total crew of one hundred and fifteen men.

Watching his commodore, Davy smiled. "Brings back some memories, doesn't it, Gabe?"

Gabe turned to face Davy. For the moment, they were friends, not a captain or commodore. "Aye, David." *SeaWolf* had been much like *Thorn*. She had been ship rigged, sleek and beautiful. The sight of *Thorn* brought back fond memories for both of them. "I want No to see her. Hex!"

"I heard you, sir. I'll make sure that he gets on board her," Hex replied.

Gabe smiled, "She is damned well armed, David. I need to go on board myself to see how she is reinforced."

"Aye, it wouldn't hurt to visit *Storm* either, Sir Gabe," David replied.

"Aye, we must maintain appearances," Gabe responded.

***

A SMOKY HAZE DRIFTED over English Harbor as the breeze shifted. The planters were burning the sugar cane fields to get ready for the harvest. Lord Randall

(Randy) Skalla walked up to the freshly painted white building at the top of the coast road.

Holding handkerchiefs to their noses, Skalla looked at his companion and said, "It doesn't seem to be so bad down at the anchorage."

The smoke was so high above Monks Hill, the sun wasn't even visible. Gabe could see a little flutter to the flag as they walked through the gate leading to Government House. It would be hot inside, Gabe knew, as the windows would all be closed, but even then, it might be cooler than outside. The marine guards that usually stood at the entrance stood just inside the doors. Gil was thinking of his men.

"Commodore," the one marine said, recognizing Gabe as a frequent guest, and being that he was the governor's brother.

Gabe returned the salute saying, "It's a bad day for the lungs and eyes, Paris."

"Aye, sir, that she be," Paris replied. The marine was happy and feeling good that the commodore had remembered his name.

A doorman walked out and, seeing Gabe, he smiled. "The governor is expecting you and the gentleman."

"Thank you, Louis. It's a lot fresher in here," Gabe responded.

"Yes sir, it is, but I guess the burning is the only way to do what they do," Louis replied.

Gabe and Lord Skalla were shown in to the governor's personal office. Skalla had taken passage on HMS *Storm*. He'd allowed the captains to make their reports yesterday before requesting to see the commodore. He would fill in the governor today on his thoughts.

After greetings and refreshments were served, Lord Skalla got down to business. "Since 1713, Great

Britain and Spain have constantly been at odds. After the seven years of war, Spain has lost vast holdings. Unfortunately, the cost of those wars was very expensive. Thinking more of replenishing the King's coffers, we attempted to tax Colonial America. Had we not done that, they'd still be flying the British flag. Rather than pay taxes, war broke out. It was one that was handled badly. Spain couldn't have cared less about the colonials winning their independence. What they saw was a possible way to win back Florida, Minorca, and most of all, the Rock of Gibraltar. With England fighting the colonials and then France, Spain saw a way to, at last, gain repossession of her lands that thus far had eluded her in war. We have found out the Bourbons had been in secret negotiations between the Colonies and France. For its part, Spain would not only take back Florida, Minorca, and the Rock of Gibraltar, but they had planned to seize Jamaica and the Bahamas. Before the end of the war, Spain had poured in so much money, especially through New Orleans, that Spanish gold was seen throughout the Colonies. At one point, when things were not going well for Britain's land war with the Colonies, Floridablanca secretly organized negotiations with Great Britain in 1780. He offered to withdraw from the war if Britain would hand over Gibraltar. We refused to do that. By the end of the war, Spain had gained nothing but a thank you from the Americans. These two ships I'm certain are to necessitate England's resources away from home and Europe. This, at a time when we have very few resources, meaning ships in service to begin with, let alone men to man them."

"I'm sure that confronting Spain would do little good," Gil said.

"To do that, would be playing into their hands, I'm afraid," Skalla answered. "Spain's hopes, I'm sure, is that we'll have to send a sizable force to deal with these ships creating havoc here. Spain will, of course, deny any knowledge of the ships. 'Can Spain be responsible for every rogue on the ocean,' will be their stance? The minute, though, that the men and ships are pulled from Gibraltar to deal with the rogues, Spain will swoop down like vultures." Skalla smiled and continued, "I haven't mentioned it to anyone but I don't doubt that they know we raided their Galleons last year and some of this is payback." Gabe and Gil agreed.

"Now gentlemen, it's been a most tiring day. I'm not as young as I used to be, so I'm for an early meal, a bath, and bed," Skalla said.

Gabe smiled at that and thought, *after being out in the smoke, I'd need a bath also*. Lord Skalla was staying with Gabe, so they'd go home together and he'd give Skalla the opportunity for the first bath.

CHAPTER TWENTY SIX

"SAIL HO!"

Gabe was trying to contain his excitement, so he waited in his cabin with Hex until the duty midshipman notified him of the sighting. Most of the officers, on deck, had gathered a respectable distance from their captain. The commodore walked on deck and Captain Davy saluted.

"From *Thorn*, sail to larboard," the lookout called down. "*Thorn* is making for flag, Cap'n. Enemy in sight."

"Alter course, Captain, to close with *Thorn*," Gabe said.

"Aye, sir," Davy replied.

"We's headed for a squall, I believe," Pittman, the master volunteered.

Captain Davy turned to Gabe, "The master said earlier that we'd hit a line of squalls before the first dog watch."

Gabe looked at his time piece; it was 3:30 p.m. Overhead, the sky was getting darker by the minute. Puerto Rico lay one hundred miles to the east of *Centaur*. Gabe had ordered *Centaur* and *Thorn* to go out on patrol.

Lord Skalla was a passenger on *Thorn*. He had put in to San Juan after seeing neither of the rogue ships in port. After saluting the flag, Skalla had used all the diplomacy he could muster, acting as if he was only alerting the Crown's friends that two ships filled with

Satan's own imps were attacking poor helpless ships and towns, deliberately and violently killing innocent women and children as well as ship's crews. He informed the mayor, who promised to relay his message to the governor, that should they need help, should those sons of hell approach San Juan, to feel free to send for help. Skalla added that a sizable force now existed to send these ships and their masters to hell.

Now as the sky darkened, the patrol headed west to pass below Hispaniola. The enemy was now sailing toward them. *Thorn* had come about and was now closing with *Centaur*.

"The Dons continue on course," the lookout called down.

"We were perhaps a day early," Captain Davy said, adding, "I think I will take a look." Climbing about half way up the near ratlines, Captain Davy focused in on the enemy ships. When he came down he said, "They are still closing. I'd have thought that they'd have seen us by now."

"They think that they can close the range with *Thorn* before we can help," Gabe said.

"I hope not," Davy replied. "Send the men to quarters, Commodore?"

"Aye, I think it is a good idea," Gabe responded.

As the pipes shrilled and the drums beat to quarters, the men went to their battle stations. Some of them were already at their guns, having heard the lookout's report.

The lookout called down again, "Dagoes 'as fired on *Thorn*."

"Any hits?" Davy asked.

"No, not as I can see, zur," the lookout replied.

"Send up our best pair of eyes," Davy ordered the first lieutenant.

"He's up there, Captain, since No made lieutenant

and left the ship," the lieutenant responded. Gabe smiled, in spite of himself.

They could see *Thorn* now, from the deck, and the roar of the enemy's guns rang out like thunder.

"When your forward gun captain feels that he is in range of the enemy, he may commence firing. Make sure that he is firing over *Thorn*. I'm sure that it would irritate her captain to have the commodore sink his ship," Gabe said. This brought laughter from those standing close by, including Captain Davy, who chuckled with the men.

The Dons fired again, however, Calvert had come up a point or two and the ball splashed into the sea.

"I believe that we are in gun range," the gunner called.

"Fire," Davy ordered.

BOOM...BOOM!!!

"Just off the bowsprit," the lookout called down after marking the shot fall.

BOOM...BOOM!!!

The forward guns on *Centaur* fired again in under two minutes. The rain started to fall, first in small drops that were hardly noticeable.

BOOM...BOOM!!!

"A hit," the lookout called down. The visibility was deteriorating, and the lookout called down, "I can't see very well, but you hit her deck."

"They're coming about," the lookout called down, just as the forward guns roared again. He squealed excitedly, "You hit her good. I saw debris flying in the air." The forward guns fired once more. "Can't see shat, Cap'n. My scope is too wet."

The wind had, in fact, picked up and a driving rain made it hard to even see the bow from the quarter-deck.

"Shall I speak to the lookout about his profanity?"

Danforth asked Davy.

"No, Lieutenant, I think the excitement and frustration caught up with him," Davy replied.

"Aye, Captain, I just don't want to encourage anyone to become lax when speaking to you," Danforth responded.

Davy stopped; *damn I wish that Dasher was still the first lieutenant,* he thought. "He'll not be the first to forget himself in the midst of a battle, Lieutenant. I believe you yourself forgot to say sir a moment ago."

"Yes, sir. Sorry, sir," the lieutenant said.

"Carry on, Lieutenant," Davy said.

"Aye, sir," the lieutenant replied.

One of the helmsmen whispered to the master, "I wish we had Lieutenant No as the first lieutenant."

"Silence," Pittman ordered.

The squall lasted an hour, but that was all the enemy ships needed to lose themselves. *Centaur* doubled back and found a spar, parts of handrails, and about half the ship's wheel, but nothing was found to indicate the ship had any more than superficial damage.

"The weather seems to favor them at every turn," Davy hissed.

With *Thorn* taking station on *Centaur*, they sailed around Cuba and then on to San Juan. They looked at the anchorage at Saint Dominica, but that was mostly French, so it didn't seem likely that the Dons would anchor there.

After the ships were not found at San Juan, Gabe decided to return to English Harbor. He'd send the next patrol up the coast of Florida, looking in at the Keys, Amelia Island, and the islands off Georgia.

The secret service officer came on board *Centaur*, once they were anchored in English Harbor. "I know it may seem trivial to you, Gabe, but you gave them a bloody nose today. That's twice that we know of that they've been damaged."

"Aye," Gabe replied. "I'm sure that they can repair themselves, though with the supplies they carry."

"I've no doubt that you are right," Skalla said, "but now it's a mind game. Except for the weather, you would have sunk one and maybe both of the rascals. Every man jack on board the two ships knows it. They can't expect to keep going unmolested, and the rogues know it."

***

THE POST CANE-HARVEST BALL was going in full swing. Most of the squadron's officers were in attendance. Greta Gardner, the wife of the dockyard commander, Admiral Gardner, was holding a glass of punch. She had made her rounds and now was talking to Gabe and Faith. As they talked, Captain David Davy walked up with Ariel. Greta saw the throng of older planter's daughters gathered around No.

"Doesn't he look distinguished in his uniform?" Greta asked. Looking at Gabe and David, she said, "I remember when two other young sailors ruled the younger hearts on the island."

"Not mine?" They turned to see Gil and Deborah walk up. "This fair lady stole my heart before we ever made English Harbor," Gil said, gently tapping Deborah's arm.

"I remember it well," Greta said, as she and Deborah embraced.

"One thing hasn't changed," Deborah said, "the boldness of those gowns."

"Why dear," Greta replied, "the women in Paris have become so independent and bold, that some of them no longer cover their breasts in public."

"Undoubtedly, some of these wenches have read the same article as you," Faith said.

"Yes, dear, you are right," Greta said. "For a poor

planter's daughter to escape the island they have to marry an Army or Naval officer."

Gil winked at Gabe and David, "Well, they are certainly advertising their product."

"Were you swooned by such women displaying themselves?" Faith asked.

"Not after I met you," Gabe answered Faith.

"He was shown the benefit of being a widow's plaything," Greta said. "Thankfully he soon realized the price was too much to pay."

"Tell the truth," Gabe said. "It only took one night. I was only a midshipman, also. I became a man very quickly."

"If any one of those girls have their way, No will find himself in some mother's clutches," Faith said. Rubbing her belly for emphasis, she added, "My condition precludes me from it, but with David's permission, Ariel, why don't you rescue No by asking him to dance."

The orchestra was just starting a new number, so Ariel said, "I will and I'll have him escort me back here."

Faith gave a big sigh, "If only Gretchen were here."

"She had the opportunity to stay," Gabe responded, not at all upset that No was getting so much attention. If nothing else, it would help the young man understand where his heart lay.

A girl dropped her fan, so she and No bent to retrieve it at the same time, resulting in an eye full for No. Ariel, almost up to them, turned and looked back their way. Faith nodded, and not a moment too soon. Of all the girls circled around No, in fact, taking into consideration all the women at the party, no one came close to matching Ariel's beauty. The possible exception was Faith.

When Ariel reached the circle, she reached out and

said, "You simply must dance with me, Noble. Did you forget your promise?"

She wrapped her arm through No's and pulled him to her, towing him to the dance floor and leaving the girls standing there.

Cecilia and Joe Moorer walked up to the group. "I believe Ariel has just incurred the wrath of several mothers," Cecilia said. She smiled and added, "I'm surprised they didn't offer to bed him."

"They just haven't gotten around to it," Joe said.

The group watched as everyone's eyes were glued to the beautiful woman and young man on the dance floor.

"That will cause a few tongues to wag, David," Gil said.

"Let them, I know where she will go home to after the party," David said.

"Let's step outside," Gil said.

"Go smoke your stinky cigars," Greta said.

"Thank you, dear, I believe we shall," Gardner said.

CHAPTER TWENTY SEVEN

AS SHOUTS AND CURSES were heard inside, Faith and Ariel rushed to the veranda to get Gabe and David. Throwing down a first class cigar, Gabe rushed to Faith, asking, "What is it?"

"No has just been challenged to a duel," Faith said.

The men all went inside. It appeared Faith's scheme to pull No from the planters' daughters had not worked as planned. When No was led to the dance floor, one of the girls, the one who had dropped her fan, felt that she had been slighted, so she went crying to her older brother. He, being a hot head, walked to where No had returned Ariel to the other women.

The brother, Luther Abercombie, walked over and touched No on the shoulder and when No turned, Luther slapped him. Luther had no way of knowing the smiling young lieutenant was a battle tested veteran from the war. No's reaction was reflexive. He knocked Luther flat on the floor. Dazed, Luther lay there for a moment. Two of his friends helped him stand up.

"You struck me, you cur," Luther said.

"What did you do to me?" No asked, the handprint and sting still on his face.

"You insulted my sister," Luther said angrily.

"Your sister wouldn't recognize an insult," No threw out.

Ariel spoke then, "I'm sorry, it was my fault. The music was already playing when I rushed in for Noble. He is not to blame."

"That could have been explained to my satisfaction had he not hit me," Luther responded.

"You struck me first," Noble said.

"A gentleman's slap," Luther said.

"It didn't feel like a gentleman's slap, but we are even so I will let it go," No replied.

A large crowd had gathered, and Luther looked around him. "Unfortunately, my honor will not allow me to let it go. I challenge you to a duel at dawn tomorrow."

"You do, and you are a dead man," No said.

Joe Moorer stepped forward and said, "Luther, this has gone on far enough. You've heard this lady accept the blame for a simple misunderstanding. Both of you struck blows, let it end there. There's no need for bloodshed."

Abercombie Senior stepped forward then. He was a hard man and was the reason that his son acted as he did. "I see this as none of your affair, Joseph."

"It is mine," Gabe said, speaking for the first time. "It is against regulations for officers to duel."

Abercombie spit on the beautiful floor, "That's what I think of your regulations. Let me tell you, sailor boy, a challenge has been issued. It will be met either on a field of honor, or in the street when their paths cross."

Vice Admiral Lord Gilbert Anthony spoke then, "As governor of this island, I will not tolerate such behavior."

Abercomhie snarled, "I'd expect that from you, but you can't protect him forever."

Lord Skalla pushed his way into the circle, and looked at the mark on No's face. He then surprised everyone. "Let them have the duel. It's obvious this fool cares very little for his son. I've seen this officer drive nails in a tree with a pistol at forty feet. He's shot a French officer between the eyes at one hundred yards, shooting up hill. If you have no regard for your son's life, let the duel proceed. I am sure the commodore was only thinking of your son when he spoke, as did the governor. And about your family, being the fool you are, you never once thought about the repercussions to your family as you egged this on. Lieutenant Noble Pride Stanhope will shoot your son dead, I've no doubt. But were he to be injured as well, as that's a direct possibility we all know. When the lieutenant's grandfather hears of your actions in this unfortunate incident, he will be most unhappy. You see, Abercombie, you have a modest plantation on Antigua, and I'm sure that like most planters, there is debt. Our young lieutenant's grandfather's holdings are larger than the entire island that we stand on. You will find no help at the bank because he will buy it. You may hang on for a short while. Your wife and daughter will give up their silk dresses and wear sacks. Hopefully, someone will pay enough for your land to pay off your mortgage. Otherwise, you will be in debtor's prison. So let's break up this little circle. I will act as the lieutenant's second and we'll see you at dawn. There is no need for a surgeon for your son, just an undertaker."

The entire crowd had gotten very quiet. Young Abercombie looked at his father and said, "You almost got me killed." He turned to Noble and said, "I apologize. You said that we were even, and you have my apology. If you still feel that way, I will leave. If you still want satisfaction I will, of course, meet you at dawn."

No looked in Luther's face, and the fear was obvious. "I accept your apology.", he said as he held out his hand. Luther shook his hand, with a big smile appearing on his face.

The orchestra started back up and people started to walk away. Joe Moorer walked over to Lord Skalla and said, "I have no way of knowing if all you said was true or not, but it certainly saved a life."

Skalla smiled, "It is true, every word of it. The Abercombie boy would have been dead tomorrow morning."

"Well, I thank you," Joe said.

Skalla looked at the man, "You are welcome, but I did it for Noble. I didn't want him to have to deal with killing a man at such a gay occasion. He's killed enough in battle already."

Joe was touched by the man's sincerity. Out of the corner of his eye, he saw the elder Abercombie catching an ear full from his wife as they walked out the door. He looked about the room and saw the young lieutenant surrounded by several young ladies and a few other young men. *Lord Skalla may not have realized it*, Joe thought, *but his words to Abercombie just made Noble the most sought after bachelor on the island.* He walked back over to his wife, "Cecilia honey, would you care to dance?"

Cecilia looked at her husband, "I thought that you'd never ask."

Back at home that night, Faith lay down next to her husband, "I apologized to Ariel. She said that I need not. She actually enjoyed the dance." Faith hesitated, "I also apologized to No. I told him that it had been my idea to get him away from those little hussies."

"Was he upset?" Gabe asked.

Faith smiled, "Not really, in fact, his words were, 'damn, I thought I looked so irresistible that Ariel couldn't help herself'. The second dance had been Ariel's idea, I told him."

Gabe replied, "We should have danced at least

once."

Faith sat up then, leaning on her elbow, "You know what he said to me, Gabe?" Without giving her husband time to ask what, Faith continued. "He told me that you were the luckiest man alive. Even in the family way, I was the most beautiful woman at the dance."

Gabe drew Faith to him, "Do I need to worry about competition?"

Faith smiled, "He worships you, Gabe Anthony. If you ever just watched him, you'd see that he does his best to emulate you. He said one more thing," Faith added, "He said had Gretchen been there, the night would have been perfect."

PART IV

The Gun Captain

The gun Cap'n yells fire
The guns leap as one
Round after round
We work 'em till we's numb

I smell the stench ó powder
It makes me cough and choke
Me eyes be burning bad
Will I stand or croak

I `ear the word cease fire
Yonder ship `as struck
I give a sigh and wipes me face
A victory cheer goes up

Michael Aye

CHAPTER TWENTY EIGHT

GRETCHEN WALKED DOWN THE stairs, overhearing the maid say that she needed money for postage due. Gretchen stood at the bottom of the steps until the mailman left. As her mother turned toward the steps, she almost collided with her daughter, not knowing that Gretchen had come down the steps.

"You've got a letter," Becky said.

Gretchen grabbed the letter and bounded up the stairs. She opened the letter, after saying a quick prayer. Her heart jumped, it at least started out promising. "My dearest love,..." Gretchen read, and then she reread the letter. *He still loves me, thank God, he still loves me.*

Gretchen spoke to her mother and father, at dinner that night. "I'm going back to Antigua."

"You can't, it's not safe. They have damned enemy ships destroying every ship that's not heavily escorted," her father said.

"It's a chance that I'll have to take. I never want to be away from No again," Gretchen replied.

"Did he ask you to come?" Becky asked.

"No, Mother. He, like you and father, worries about the damn Dagoes," Gretchen said.

Her mother's mouth dropped, "Watch your mouth, young lady."

"Why, you don't think that I've not heard you... and father curse at times. I'm a grown woman. I acted like a spoiled child, which I've been all my life. It has broken my heart, and I've suffered dearly. Thank God, No still loves me in spite of it. I'm going back. I can be as much of a woman as Faith and Ariel are."

"Let Gabe, at least, put an end to those...damn Dagoes first," Becky said.

"Three months, Mother. Three months and then I'm going. I shall write No tonight," Gretchen replied.

***

SCURRY BIRDS RAN BACK and forth on the beach following the water as it washed up and then receded. A pelican sat on an overturned boat, lazing away in the sun. A few gulls hovered over the ships, waiting for some morsels to be thrown overboard.

Gabe sat in the commodore's great cabin with his dispatches. "According to the Admiralty, there have been three mail packets lost. Two of them before they reached Barbados, and the other one after it left Bermuda."

"That is out of our patrol area," Captain Laqua threw out.

"This is true," the commodore responded, "but they've only got one frigate and a brig, and are not making any progress, as we are."

"It's like looking for the proverbial needle in a haystack," Captain Honeycutt volunteered.

"Aye, we've started at both ends of the patrol area and meet in the middle, without sighting the bloody buggers," Captain Bahnsen agreed. The other captains all agreed.

"I think that after catching fire from *Centaur* they found a hole to hide in," Captain Troy said. "They are now attacking outside of our normal areas."

"I agree, so we will change up," Gabe said. "We will send two ships to make the usual patrol. Spies will see us and the word may get passed to the Dagoes. We will then send two more ships to patrol the convoy routes from Tobago south to Cape Verde. Captain Bedford, you and Captain Calvert will take that route. If you need charts, get with *Centaur's* master. Captain Bahnsen and Captain Honeycutt, you will take the usual patrol but look in at Sanibel and Marco Island."

"Aye, there were some fishing boats near Captiva last time we were in that area. They might have seen something," this coming from Bahnsen. Gabe nodded his head in the affirmative.

"Let's not forget Key West either," Honeycutt said. "Those fishermen promised to be on the lookout."

"Captain Skidmore," Gabe said, "I will shift my flag to *Warlock* and, together with Captain Laqua, we will patrol the mail route."

"We will be honored, sir," Troy said. Gabe smiled and thought, *he's probably thinking 'why in the hell did he choose me.'*

"When do we get underway?" Troy asked.

"Tomorrow is Thursday, and with the sailor's superstitions being what they are, we'd probably have a mutiny if we sailed tomorrow. So we will sail Saturday morning," Gabe said. The meeting was adjourned then.

Gabe called to his servant, "Josh, pack a box of food and wine to take over to *Warlock*. I know Captain Skidmore has not been given anything but partial pay for a while."

"Aye, Sir Gabe," Josh replied. He knew the commodore meant to not only take enough, but a bit extra. "Will there be lieutenants dining as well?"

"Possibly," Gabe responded.

"I will pack accordingly then, sir." Josh thought as he turned, *Sir Gabe would invite all the lieutenants just to have the opportunity to dine with young Noble.*

When everything was quiet, Hex walked up, "Doctor Honeycutt peered in and saw the meeting going on, so he left. He went on shore so he may have been going to check on Faith."

"How far along is she," Gabe said, thinking aloud.

"Six months, I believe," Josh said from the pantry.

Gabe and Hex looked at each other and then smiled. "Damme, Josh," Gabe said, "I believe that you could hear a flea fart." They all laughed again.

***

SATURDAY MORNING, GABE AND Faith sat at the table. Izzie, the new cook, had learned her master and his wife liked to sit together in the early morning. Sometimes over breakfast, and at other times like today, they just had coffee. She listened at the door, not to eavesdrop, but to see if they needed anything.

Jake Hex, that big old cox'n, had already gone to the ship. "Tell Sir Gabe that I'll be ready when he gets to the waterfront."

Lum had taken Hex down to the harbor and was back now with the carriage. Lum sat in the kitchen finishing off a biscuit coated with honey and butter. Biscuits were the first thing that Nanny had taught to her to make, and not long after that she had learned to fix several other types of what Nanny called, 'food fit for the Lawd.'

Izzie worked for the carpenter's wife until she died. The carpenter sold his business to his apprentice and then moved to Virginia. Working with Nanny was much different than working with a woman who was old and sick all the time.

Lum finished his food, and drank down the last swallow of coffee. He then walked into the breakfast room. "It's about time, sir."

Gabe looked at his timepiece. How the devil did Lum always know when it was time? He didn't have a timepiece and, to Gabe's knowledge, he didn't know how to read one if he did. After embracing Faith, he walked out to the carriage where Lum was waiting.

Hex had his boat ready at the waterfront and he was rowed over to *Warlock*. Before the bow man hooked onto the chain, Gabe could see faces looking off the side, and the blue and white uniform of an officer.

"Boat ahoy!" came the challenge from on board *Warlock*.

"Flag," Hex replied, and then said, "toss yer oars."

The bow man hooked the chains as Gabe stood in the stern sheets. Hex offered a hand but Gabe ignored it and stepped onto the tumble home and up the battens, and then through the entry port. Pipes shrilled forth, and the fifes and drums beat forth as Captain Skidmore stepped forward to welcome the commodore. His pennant was raised and, catching the wind, it flapped a time or two, and then stood out.

Looking up at the flag, and then back to the commodore, Troy spoke, "You honor us, Sir Gabe." Whether to show off his skills or trying to impress the commodore, Troy called, "Mr. Stanhope, you may get us underway. Would you like to go below, sir?"

"I believe that I will watch your crew, if you don't mind, Captain," Gabe replied.

"By all means, sir, I've always found it exciting to get underway. It can tell a captain a lot about his crew."

"And his officers," Gabe added.

Gabe watched as Noble got the men moving and the ship underway. He saw the master lean over and speak to Noble a couple of times, but before he knew it *Warlock* was sliding out into the open water with Fort Berkeley falling astern. Eight bells rang out and the forenoon watch replaced the morning watch. There were a good many already on deck and ready to take over as getting underway hands were relieved and the watch set. Gabe, going below to get out of the men's way, was shown to a chair in the captain's cabin.

"Would you prefer a cup of coffee or cocoa?" Troy asked.

"Whichever you prefer, Captain," Gabe replied.

"I think cocoa. Felix," Troy called out, "bring the commodore and me a cup of cocoa."

***

SEVERAL COASTAL TRADERS WERE seen headed toward Barbados. The little traders hopped from island to island to earn a meager profit. They flew no flag and even during the war they were rarely boarded unless there was suspicion of them working against the Crown. None of the little traders reported seeing anything of the Spanish ships.

It was morning of the third day at sea that Barbados was sighted by the lookout. On a clear day, Needham's Point could be seen about ten leagues out. Felix, being new to the navy, asked what a league is.

Hex looked at the man and smiled, "If I remember correctly, one nautical league equals about three and a half miles, or close to it."

"Why don't they just say that?" Felix asked.

"Because the navy has its own way, mate," Hex replied.

"I see," Felix said, but it was obvious that the little man did not.

The white powder beaches stood out at a distance, as they neared the island. Numerous ships were at anchor in Carlisle Bay, with most of them being East Indiaman. There was only one naval frigate visible.

"We need to find out if they are coming or going," Gabe said.

Captain Skidmore nodded, "I'm sure that you will pay your respects to the governor. While you do that,

I'll speak with the captain of the escort frigate."

"Good idea," Gabe responded.

"When do you want to sail?" Troy asked.

"Tomorrow morning, God willing," Gabe replied.

CHAPTER TWENTY NINE

HMS *WARLOCK* AND HMS *Active* set sail the following morning. The only information Gabe was able to gain was that a friend of the governor, Matthew Payne, had sent a letter that he would sail within a fortnight. It had arrived two weeks ago, and he had scheduled passage in the mail packet, *Lady Gail.* This meant that he should have arrived six to eight weeks after the letter was posted. It wasn't a lot of help, but it made Gabe think that his plan of action was the right one.

In the early pre-dawn hours the day after sailing from Barbados, Jake Hex woke Sir Gabe. "I have a pot of coffee if you would like some, sir."

Gabe swung around and found his britches. Once he got those on and stomped his feet home in his boots, he picked up his shirt and walked to the table. His toothbrush and brushing powder were laid out. He would brush his teeth after quarters. He'd slept badly last night. He'd awakened several times thinking of Dagan. He sipped his coffee and slipped his shirt on. After another sip of coffee, Gabe noticed the sugar and a jar of honey on the table with a spoon. He'd not gotten into the habit of sweetening his coffee yet.

"Commodore, would you like to have a shave now or later?" Jake asked.

Gabe rubbed his chin, and looked at Jake, "What time is it?"

"You have time," the cox'n replied.

Felix already had the bowl and a towel in his hand. Gabe took a larger sip of coffee as Felix set out a container of Vroom and Fowler's walnut oil military shaving soap. Opening the container, he took out a bar, wet it and lathered Gabe's face. Within five minutes, the shave was completed and Felix splashed a bit of liquid on Gabe's face.

Felix said, looking at Gabe, "This is a balm to soothe the face, in case of razor burn. I've learned the wind can be irritating, so the balm used after shaving helps both. It is made from oil of peppermint, or sweet almond oil mixed in rose water. If the face is very irritated a small amount of aloe and rosemary is now being used by some men and smells nice."

Gabe felt that he'd been given a lesson in caring for the face. The coffee was very good, as was the meal last evening. As they went on deck, Gabe said to Hex, "That does make your face feel good."

"It smells nice too," Jake said, adding, "Captain Skidmore has himself a rare find."

Gabe was greeted by Captain Skidmore as he walked to the quarterdeck. He did not miss the slight nod or finger to the nose by No. He was a friend but that didn't stop him from alerting his captain that the commodore was near. This pleased Gabe. The boy had done very well in learning his way about a ship. Most of it had to do with an eagerness to learn and the ability to show respect and appreciation to a man, regardless of his station in life or on board ship.

Gabe still was not sure if he'd have recommended him for promotion this early, but he had to admit that No had handled the increase in responsibility well. He had certainly grown with the promotion thanks to Captain Skidmore and Paul Johns, the first lieutenant.

Gabe realized, looking about the ship, that it would be a few minutes before the sky was light enough for the lookouts to see. Dawn was a time when the enemy could be broadside to you without you realizing it. When the sun started to rise, it did so quickly. The faces of the men at the quarterdeck became clearer, and then the bow was suddenly visible.

It was only a few minutes before the lookout called down, "*Active* be on station, Cap'n. Horizon be clear." *A clear concise report*, Gabe thought, *with no unnecessary words.*

"Dismiss the hands from quarters, Mr. Johns," the captain said.

"Aye, Captain," Johns replied.

Troy then spoke to the commodore, "The master predicts contrary winds this morning." Gabe nodded, not doubting the master.

The wind soon decreased and died completely. The sea was like glass and the sun hot, as it bore down on the ship. Occasionally, a sail would flap, causing everyone to look at it, but it would only be a brief breeze.

"Do we put the longboats out and tow the ship?" the first lieutenant asked. Troy shook his head no, as the men were just going to breakfast.

After another hour, the sails began to flap and snap. "The wind," the master shouted, "the wind." *Warlock* was soon gliding along.

"*Active* be on station," the lookout called down again.

A cast of the log showed *Warlock* making ten knots through the water. Gabe caught a glimpse of No near the bow with his hat off and the wind blowing his hair straight back.

"The lad is enjoying the moment, Sir Gabe," Troy said.

Gabe smiled, "He is at that, Troy."

Gabe saw Hex and Finch over by the companion ladder. He then saw someone just inside the companionway. It was the master, and he was very animated in his discussion. Making his way to the companion ladder, Gabe spoke to Hex, "You are not causing any mischief, are you?"

Hex smiled, "Graves said he thought that we'd have a calm by 8:00. Finch asked if he meant 8:00 this morning, or 8:00 tonight. Graves didn't think that was funny."

"I trust old Graves," Finch said. "I was just japing."

Gabe noticed a sudden difference in the ship. "So you were just japing?"

"Aye, sir, I swear," Finch replied.

"I'm glad to hear it, since the wind just dropped again," Gabe said. Finch's mouth gaped as Gabe moved so that he could see the slack sails.

Warlock's bosun, Mr. Christie was as profane a man as Gabe had ever met. He was also a huge bulk of a man. His bosun's pipe hung around a neck so thick that it looked like it strained the pipe's lanyard. His uniform had paint stains that overlapped other stains. He was slapping a starter against the side of his leg as he cursed the sky, the water, and some slackard. "Ye'll be put in a longboat by yer lonesome, towing this lady until we reach Portsmouth, you sorry excuse for…for, I can't even think of nothing sorry as ye be. Yer lower than whale shat, Palmer. You stink worse than a whore's drawers after her monthly curse."

Gabe walked away, not hearing it all, but undoubtedly it was something to do with hygiene as he saw men drawing buckets of sea water up.

In the captain's cabin, Hex pointed towards a chair where a cup of coffee was waiting. "The odors on board a ship has never smelled like lilacs, but when a man smells so bad that others don't want him in the mess, it's really bad," Hex said.

A commotion was heard on deck, followed by a scream and a curse. There was a midshipman being announced soon after that. "Mr. Hartley's respects sir, he thinks that you need to come on deck."

Gabe got up and walked out. Hex followed a respectful distance away. Finch walked up to Gabe and Troy. "It appears that the man, Palmer, isn't no man at all. He's a she! One man and the bosun were in front with a bucket of sea water. While they had his...her attention, another seaman made his way behind her and ripped the smelly shirt off. When he did, teats flopped loose. She's got them backed off now with a wicked blade."

Palmer put down the knife as Troy spoke to her. Noble walked up with some seaman's top. Palmer had her arms crossed trying to keep her breasts covered.

Speaking softly, No said, "Why don't you turn so that you are looking outboard and I'll hand you this top. You put it on, and then go forward. You are in my division, aren't you?"

The girl nodded and put the top on, and then walked forward as instructed. The men held their heads down as she passed them.

"Permission to question Palmer, sir," Noble said.

The captain and first lieutenant were standing together, but it was the captain who spoke, "Proceed, Mr. Stanhope, and then report to me...and Mr. Johns after you are through."

Noble returned an hour later, and the marine sentry announced, "First lieutenant to see the captain, and the third lieutenant to see the captain, sir."

Gabe said, "At least, he didn't bust the butt plate on the deck." Troy looked at Gabe and smiled.

"Robert Palmer is, in fact, Roberta Palmer," No reported. "She got picked up by a press gang. She was trying to work her father's boat when the press gang mistook her for a man. She'd always helped her father and knew her way around a ship so she went along with it. Her father had just died and she was having a rough go of it. She'd at least eat on board ship. She's only seventeen, sir," Noble said. "Normally, she'd have been able to bathe on shore, but things hadn't worked out for her to get on shore lately. Being young and smallish, she was still able to pull her own weight."

"The question is what do we do with her now?" Troy asked. "It's one thing to sleep with a bunch of horny sailors when you're supposed to be a man. It's too risky now that they know she's a woman."

"I've a couple of recommendations, Captain." Troy looked at Noble as if to say go on. "Sir, Jimmy Ducks is near too feeble to carry on, so Palmer could help his wife with the livestock and sleep in their space as well." Jimmy Ducks was the man who cared for the animals on board the ship until they were slaughtered for food. His wife's name was Olga. "The other plan is to make her an assistant for the surgeon."

Troy looked at Noble, "Good thoughts, Lieutenant. Mr. Johns, do you have a preference?"

"No, sir, I'd talk to the surgeon first, before you offer that," Johns replied.

"Well...," Noble started, "Robert Palmer has been hanging with the surgeon in his...ere her off duty time. I don't think that it will matter to Pilcher if Palmer...if he's a he or a she."

"I will leave it in your capable hands, Lieutenant, but see if one of the mids have something better that she can wear."

"Aye, Captain," Noble replied.

CHAPTER THIRTY

THE NOON MEAL HAD been served and the crew lay about, gathered in areas that offered even a slight shade. Under a blazing sun, the little spaces that offered any comfort were growing smaller. A few of the men kicked around the conversation about having a woman among them for months and not even realizing it. That conversation soon dried up though. A scuttlebutt had been hauled up on deck, and the men stood in line waiting on their turn at the dipper.

Felix had retrieved a bottle of hock from the bilges. It was much cooler down there, and he had been tempted to take a nap but the smell was so that he came back up. A glass was poured for the captain and commodore.

"Help yourself to a glass, Felix," Captain Skidmore said.

"Thank you, Captain," Felix responded. He wondered, when he was back in the pantry, if the captain had caught a whiff of his breath where he'd already taken a taste of the hock. *It was a better brand than what the governor used to drink,* he thought as he poured himself a glass and took a drink.

Voices rang out overhead, "The wind, she blows... she blows." *It's back*, Gabe thought thankfully.

Captain Skidmore gave a big grin and rushed from the cabin, colliding with the midshipman of the watch and sending him sprawling. The marine sentry and the captain both bent over to lift the dazed Mr.

Buntin up.

"My apologies, young sir," Troy said as he picked up the mid's hat.

Lieutenant Noble Stanhope smiled, "You'll forego charges this time for striking an officer, won't you, Captain?"

Troy was taken aback for a moment and heard the commodore laugh. Cheeky...the new lieutenant has a cheeky side about him as well, yet it was funny. "Aye, Lieutenant, if you'll speak on his behalf, we'll hold off on his kissing the gunner's daughter this time."

Young Buntin was a bit frightened, but seeing the smiling faces, he felt that all was as it should be.

"Let's go on deck, shall we," Troy said. He moved to the side and said, "You first, Mr. Buntin. Lieutenant Stanhope, make sure the path topside is clear."

"Aye, Captain," Stanhope replied.

On deck, there was a definite breeze that could be felt. Most of the crew stood about as the canvas flapped about in the wind. A sound, not unlike that of a musket going off, was heard and the sails filled.

"Let's be about it," Noble called to the bosun.

Within minutes, HMS *Warlock* and HMS *Active* were full and by. Had the lost time made any difference? Gabe hoped not, but no one could say for sure.

It was late in the first dogwatch that the lookout called down, "Sails off the bow." In less than a minute, he called down again. "It be a convoy, Cap'n."

Captain Skidmore turned to Gabe, "Bait, Commodore?"

"Possibly," Gabe replied.

A corner began to flap noisily on the main sail. The second lieutenant, Mr. Hartley, called to the bosun, who was near. "I believe that you have a foot loose there, Mr. Tabby."

"Aye ,sir, I just saw it," Tabby said. Calling to one of

his mates, the bosun assigned the repairs.

The convoy was upon them within the hour. They reported that none of their convoy had been molested. Two strange sails did close with the convoy though, until two of the escort ships, both frigates belonging to the Bombay Marines, had come about and showed their open gun ports.

"It sounds like we could be right this time, Sir Gabe," Troy said.

"Aye, Troy, but hearing about them and bringing them to battle are not the same," Gabe replied.

Troy agreed with him. Nobody knew better than he unless it was young Noble Stanhope, that the commodore's reputation was on the verge of being tarnished. Nothing in the past mattered, not all the victories, the ships captured, or the taking of the treasure ships. No, his success had made a lot of men jealous, including some of the higher ups in the Admiralty. While they sat on their fat arses and benefited from what men like the commodore did, they had no idea of what it took to lead men into combat. Most of them had never been in battle where the next second a ball may strike your skull and kill you outright, or suffer a splinter as big as your arm through the gut where you lay agonizingly, praying for a quick death. No, they saw men with limbs missing, but the hell they went through when they lost a limb never occurred to most people. He'd heard a former captain say every politician needed to be a veteran of some battle before they had the ability to declare war. There was no doubt a few of them would change their voting habits.

***

IT WAS A CLEAR starry night. The ship was under easy sail with a soldier's wind. On the main deck, men sat back and listened to Hex play and sing. The nagging feeling that Gabe had felt not long ago was back. It had come upon him after dinner.

Felix was nearly as good as Josh Nesbit when it came to cooking. They had dined on steak with carrots, spring greens, and pureed potatoes, and also gravy to pour over the steak and potatoes. For dessert, an apple pie was set on the table. With the surgeon and first lieutenant as guests, a second helping of the apple pie had not been available.

Captain Skidmore had dipped into his wine chest and brought out a bottle of Bourgogne red wine. Smiling, he said, "A case of this was given to me by the American doctor who first tended to my wounds." Taking a sip of his wine, Troy Skidmore thought of Joan Heard, his nurse from America. They had written to each other, but would it come to be more? He sure missed the cool, gentle way her hands felt on his body when he woke up after being brought on shore in Norfolk, Virginia.

She had been changing his dressings. Thinking that he was asleep, she had leaned over and kissed his lips. He opened his eyes and seeing him awake, she smiled. He had wanted her, wanted her badly, but was too hurt and weak to carry the relationship further.

After dinner, when he could politely do so, Gabe went topside and talked with No. Hex watched them. He knew that Gabe and Faith cared for Noble Pride Stanhope like a son. Hex felt something towards the boy…like a son? He didn't know, but his feelings towards No were strong. Like Gabe, Hex had a nagging feeling about what tomorrow would bring. With his guitar in hand, he walked towards the captain's cabin to put the guitar away. Felix Smith smiled and spoke, but Hex just walked on by. *Please Lord, see us through tomorrow*, he prayed.

***

THE DAWN HORIZON HAD proved to be clear. It was just after 10:00 a.m. when the men on deck stopped. Several of them had heard it...gunfire! The first lieutenant called to the duty midshipman to let the captain know what sounded like gunfire had been heard.

Shouting, he called up to the lookout, "Can you see anything?"

"No, sir," the lookout replied.

"How in the hell can we hear it and you not see it," the first lieutenant responded.

"I'll go up," Noble volunteered.

"I wish that you would," the first lieutenant said. "The man is undoubtedly blind."

Noble made it to the main tops and after some focusing, he saw the sails of a small ship trying her best to out run a ship firing at her. He was about to call out his report when he saw another ship a few miles in front. The packet, if that's what she was, was running right into the waiting ship's guns. Catching a backstay, Noble slid to the deck. He quickly explained what he saw to the first lieutenant, with the captain and commodore listening also.

"Clamp on all she'll carry," Troy ordered. "We'll get the sodomites this time." he said. His sail drills paid off. The crew had the extra sails on in no time. "Mr. Johns, beat to quarters, if you will."

Gabe approved of the way Troy handled his ship. There was no wasted time asking the commodore's permission.

A grizzled old sailor spoke to No, "Think we'll be on time to save the packet, Mr. Stanhope?"

"I don't know, Oswald, but it will be close," No replied.

Gabe smiled, it did the old sailor good for Noble to speak to him and had even remembered his name.

If more officers learned that respect was a two way street, the Royal Navy would have less desertion. This was something that Gabe's father had instilled in both Gil and Gabe.

CHAPTER THIRTY ONE

WARLOCK WAS OUTDISTANCING ACTIVE, but Captain Laqua knew, as did the commodore, that to save the packet time was of the essence. The packet had spotted the ship off her bow. It was too late, but the captain had sailed to starboard. He wouldn't outsail the Dons, but they'd have to follow her to get the guns to bear again. Once the forward ship changed course to intercept the packet, the captain changed course again. The enemy had fired again, but not one of their balls struck home.

"Come on girl, fly," the master of the packet whispered to his ship.

The packet ship changed again and by the count of twenty, he went back to his original course. The head frigate lost time trying to readjust. The packet's trick had worked once, but it was unlikely that it would work again. The roar of cannons sounded again. One ball landed close to the packet's bow this time. Another went through her sails.

They were now close to the range of the bow chaser, so Captain Skidmore yelled, "Mr. Christie, you may fire when ready."

"Aye, Cap'n," Christie bellowed his reply.

It was like watching a terrier dog after a rat, Gabe thought. The enemy's gun thundered and a twenty-four pound ball hit the ship in the stern.

"That's put paid to that game," a sailor called out, knowing the packet was likely doomed.

Christie, however, now felt good about his range, firing the larboard and then the starboard bow chasers. It crashed down on the larboard beam of the Dago frigate.

"I think that you hit a gun," the lookout called down.

"It damn well got their attention," Lieutenant Johns quipped.

Christie kept firing the cannons...a miss, a hit, and then another miss.

"They've at least left the packet alone," Troy volunteered.

The Dons' frigate had now turned to meet *Warlock*.

"Standby men, she'll fire any moment," Troy said.

An entire broadside was let go from the *Tigress*. Sails were pockmarked, and balls fell on either side, but *Warlock* suffered no hits.

Christie kept firing *Warlock's* guns, and the lookout finally yelled down, "She be turning away, Captain."

"Run today and live to fight another day," the master said.

Gabe said, "Not today."

The distance was much closer now. The forward guns, all that could be brought to bear, fired almost simultaneously.

The lookout in the tops was jumping up and down shouting excitedly. He could see beyond the smoke. "The whole damn stern be gone," he shouted. "Her rudder is certainly shot away."

"Aye," Troy said, "but don't forget that she still has teeth. Laqua will not like it but signal *Active* to take charge of that ship. Shall we fire as we pass?"

"I see no reason not to," Gabe answered. He then added, "Damn their Dago souls."

The enemy ship fired just as *Warlock* passed. If

there had been any doubt in regards to punishing the ship, that act of defiance removed it.

"Fire as long as a gun will bear," Troy shouted down to Noble, who was in charge of the gun deck.

The deck shook after each of *Warlock's* eighteen pounders poured their deadly destruction into the ship. The Spanish seamen, seeing flames spew forth from *Warlock's* side, ran but there was no escaping the hell being poured on them. When the last gun had fired, Gabe turned to see figures jumping up and down and waving on the mail packet.

"I think that you may secure the guns for now, Captain. The frigate is done for. Laqua can pick up any survivors if he chooses after the packet has received his attention. I also want a good set of eyes of yonder ship," Gabe said, pointing to the fleeing ship.

"Aye, Sir Gabe."

It was a good four or five hours until dark. Hopefully, they'd catch up to her by then. The men were given a ration of rum.

"It's on the commodore, lads," Captain Skidmore told the crew. He then smiled at Gabe, "So our purser won't whine." Gabe grinned at Troy.

"We mustn't let that happen," Gabe japed.

The lookout was changed every hour. After three hours it was obvious, even from the quarterdeck, that they were overtaking the enemy ship.

"We'll catch her," Lieutenant Hartley said to Noble as he relieved the second lieutenant at 4:00 p.m., or 1600.

The chase continued but now the xebec frigate was much closer. It was close enough that vague shapes on deck could be made out.

The lookout called down, "They's got two women standing on the taffrail. It looks like 'e's going to shoot them or cast 'em over the side."

"Shooting them won't slow us down," Gabe said. "He'll toss them into the sea."

"There have been too many lives lost to worry about two girls," the first lieutenant remarked.

"Put a boat over with two volunteers that can swim," Gabe said. "They'll have to cut the pulley ropes, so give them sharp axes."

"I can swim," Noble volunteered.

Captain Troy shook his head no. "We need you on the gun deck, sir."

Midshipman Rawls stepped forward. "I'm an excellent swimmer, sir."

"And I also," one of the bosun's mates declared.

"Swing out the boat," Troy ordered. Thinking of his near death in the water, Troy spoke again, "Get a hatch cover ready to toss over in case something happens to the boat."

Hex and Finch helped the men in the ship's boat. "Chop the stern rope first or you'll be arse over tea kettle."

"Aye, sir."

"Don't chop the ropes until we give the signal. But once given, you must act quickly or you'll be swamped. Put the oars down inside the boat."

"Yes, sir," Rawls replied. The boy was a bit pale but determined.

"Us'll do it," Harris, the bosun's mate said. *Warlock* continued to close the gap.

"If the women were not on the stern, we could fire the bow chasers," Captain Skidmore said, thinking aloud.

"Aye," the master responded, "but dark will be on us in less than an hour."

The master had voiced what had been on Gabe's mind for the last few minutes. "Send for the marine lieutenant," Gabe ordered.

"Here I am," marine Lieutenant Dartmouth responded on hearing his name.

"Do you have any marksmen, Lieutenant? I mean true marksmen," Gabe asked.

"I've got one that I'd put up against anyone," Dartmouth replied.

"Put him on the bow, and when we get in range, I want him to shoot the rogue standing by the girls," Gabe said.

"Aye, Sir Gabe. He could do it on land, but at sea, it might prove chancy."

Gabe replied, "The ship has a steady feel. He could shoot when he feels that he has got it."

"Yes, sir," the lieutenant responded.

"They could fire their stern guns now," Christie said. "Why are they holding back?"

"That would cost them the protection of those girls," Captain Skidmore answered.

"*La Cazadora*," the master said, "does anyone know what that means?"

"The *Huntress*," Noble said from where he stood by the ladder to the gun deck. Seeing Troy look at him, Noble continued, "Rawls is in the boat, Captain."

"Send Mr. Padgett to act as messenger for the gun deck," the captain ordered.

Damn, Johns thought, *I should have thought of that already*.

"Mr. Christie!"

"Aye, Commodore."

"When the sharpshooter fires, I expect those girls to jump. Give it the count of five, and if they don't jump, go ahead and fire into the ship's stern. Have someone ready to signal which side the girls jump to. Hopefully, we can avoid them."

"Yes sir, Commodore," Christie replied.

Hex looked at Gabe and said, "They'll jump, sir.

They want to be away from that hell."

"I hope you are right, Jake, but either way, we'll fire. Too many lives have been lost to these whoresons already."

Nobody spoke, but they all knew the commodore was right. The time was short and they couldn't let *La Cazadora* escape. Some would have already fired thinking the two girls were a small price to pay...and indeed it was, but the fat little coastal trader, Pepe would not think so.

Captain Skidmore must have been reading Gabe's thoughts. "No one could blame you, Sir Gabe. It's a hard choice, but one that has to be made."

BANG!!!

"Damn," Troy cursed.

The sharpshooter had been given an opportunity and fired. The Don fell. The men on *Warlock's* bow were shouting, "Jump, jump!"

It was doubtful that the girls could hear, but they could see the men on *Warlock* making diving motions. Another man was running towards them. The girls grabbed each other's hands and jumped.

"To starboard," the man at the bow shouted. "They jumped to starboard."

"Larboard," Troy yelled, "Hard over."

As the order was given, the main hatch cover was cast over. That was all they could physically do for now.

"Damn, we should have put a lantern in the boat," Troy cursed again.

"We did, Cap'n," Finch replied.

CHAPTER THIRTY TWO

WARLOCK'S BOW CHASERS FIRED. They had fired, even as the helmsman followed the captain's orders. Even changing directions, parts of the stern disintegrated into flying splinters. La Cazadora's stern chasers fired as well, but missed entirely as Warlock's helm shifted.

Christie was cursing and pushing his men to sponge out, load, and fire. This time, the stern windows were shattered and a gaping hole filled the entire stern section of *La Cazadora*. Suddenly, the enemy captain luffed.

"Damn," Troy shouted. "Everyone down...down," he shouted.

The captain of *La Cazadora* knew his business. By luffing, *Warlock* was quickly alongside the enemy, who fired ball after twenty-four pound ball into *Warlock's* hull. The crew felt their ship shudder as the enemy balls hit. However, not every ball hit. Some of them screamed as they flew overhead.

Noble, without waiting to be ordered, had *Warlock's* guns firing as each gun came to bear. As the sky was darkening, the orange flames seemed very bright as the cannons from each ship fired. On the forecastle, Christie had the carronades blasting away. The recoil seemed to be vibrating down the deck planks. Overhead riggings were falling. A block and tackle fell hitting one of Christie's gunners, spattering blood and brains over the gun. Christie grabbed the man's body as if it were nothing and flung it over the side.

"Don't stand there like old women, fire," he yelled, "Fire, damn you, fire!"

The carronade fired again. *Warlock* slid past *La Cazadora*. The stern guns on *Warlock* were answering the bow guns on the enemy ship.

"Prepare to come about," Captain Skidmore ordered the first lieutenant.

"Aye, sir," the lieutenant responded.

The crews for sail handling answered the bosun's call. They had outdistanced the Dons.

"We'll not have much longer," the master informed his captain.

"Ready, Captain," Lieutenant John's reported.

"Ready!" Troy shouted. "About!"

The ship went through the maneuver in a timely fashion. Gabe had heard the master's comments. He looked at the sky. There was no sign of *Active*. It would have been nice had she been there, but she wasn't.

"Troy," Gabe called to Captain Skidmore. "We'll pass one more time and come about. Fire every gun double shotted, and the guns on the forecastle and quarterdeck arm with grape on top of ball. If the Dagoes haven't surrendered, we'll grapple with the sons of Satan. I would just as soon as blast them to hell, but if we have to grapple to keep from losing them, we will." *It's too late for armbands*, Gabe thought, *but the men should recognize their mates*.

Captain Skidmore called to the marine lieutenant, "Have the men in the tops firing canister down on the Dago's quarterdeck."

"Aye, Captain," he responded.

The ships were almost upon each other when a nervous gunner jerked the lanyard on *La Cazadora*. Other gunners followed so that half of the broadside fired before a single gun could bear.

"We've got them scared," Troy laughed, letting off a bit of nervousness himself.

"'Ere that lads, the cap'n said we done 'skerd' 'em," a sailor said.

Men laughed and others cheered. Johns went to silence them, but Gabe spoke out, "Let them cheer, Lieutenant, maybe it will frighten the Dons even more."

The gun deck started firing at that time. Not a broadside all at once, but each gun in succession, every ball hitting the rogue ship. Several of the eighteen pound balls hit the enemy gun ports, knocking guns over, and hurling them back on their crew. One of the enemy guns' powder bag exploded as a ball hit it, as it was in the process of being loaded. Across the way, screams and curses could be heard as *Warlock's* guns and swivels found targets.

All of the enemy guns were not silent, though. One of the enemy's shots tore the first lieutenant in half, and beheaded the master. A portion of *Warlock's* wheel was hit and a helmsman died. The wheel began to spin, but Hex jumped in to help the surviving helmsman. The two ships ground together and slid past each other as the wind pushed the ships along.

"Lieutenant Hartley," Captain Troy called.

The bosun, Tabby, answered, "He's done for, Captain."

"Prepare to come about, Mr. Tabby. You'll have to take Hartley's place."

"Aye, Cap'n," Tabby replied.

"Mr. Buntin," Troy called. "You are acting lieutenant, help Mr. Tabby."

"Aye, sir," Buntin replied.

Troy walked to the gun deck ladder. "Mr. Stanhope, fire into the enemy as we come together, and then bring your men on deck to board the damn Dagoes. Send someone to get your weapons."

"Aye, Captain."

A barrel of cutlasses had been brought over next to the ladder, and Noble yelled, "gun captains, make sure your men arm themselves on the way topside."

"Aye, Mr. No," they replied. No smiled, someone had heard of his nickname.

Tabby had the sails off *Warlock*, as the ships closed, so that she wouldn't push past the enemy. Christie fired all the forecastle guns that would bear. The enemy's stern guns were silent. *Was that luck or an omen*, Gabe wondered. *Had the enemy captain planned something more ominous?*

Gabe looked at Troy, "Handle your ship, Captain, and I'll lead the boarders. Lieutenant Dartmouth, have your sharpshooters focus on the Don's men in the tops, and the men at the swivels sweep the decks. I want, at least, two rounds on that deck before we board."

"Aye, sir," Dartmouth responded.

Warlock's bow sprit was now even with the stern of *La Cazadora*. This will be it, Gabe thought. His mind suddenly was on Faith.

He turned to Hex, "If I should fall, Jake."

"Clear your mind, Sir Gabe. If you fall, I shall already have fallen."

This time, there were no nervous hands on the lanyard on *La Cazadora*. Both ships fired, with *Warlock* firing a full broadside, but less than half of that by the Dons. Muskets rang out from *Warlock's* tops followed by another crash as the swivels fired.

Gabe saw men on board the Dago ship fall from the tops. One man fell into a group that was ready to repel boarders. Grapnels were heaved, and men on the enemy ship ran to chop at the lines, but the swivels crashed out again, killing them.

Seamen on *Warlock* heaved on the grapnel lines pulling the two ships together. Gabe watched as a grapnel hook had caught a man in the back. The hooks went through him as it bit into the wall of the ship's side. In the tops, more muskets rang out. The hulls ground together and, just as Gabe was about to send the boarders over, the swivels crashed out again. The flash had momentarily blinded Gabe, as it had gotten dark.

"Boarders away," he yelled. "Go at them, lads. Make them pay for our men. Remember *Nimble*," Gabe yelled.

The roar of the men nearly shattered Gabe's eardrums, as they went up and over to the enemy's deck. As he climbed on the rail to swing over, Gabe was taken aback at all the dead bodies scattered across the deck. Many of them were stacked on top of their mates.

Gabe was met by a Spanish sailor as he made the enemy deck. The man was running after him, with his blade held back ready to swing forward. Suddenly, the man stopped. His hand went to his head, as much of his skull was missing, as one of *Warlock's* sharpshooters had shot him.

Men yelled, cursed, and cried out in pain as the boarders pressed forward. It was a general melee now. Gabe could see many of *Warlock's* men fall but there were more of the enemy falling. Gabe found himself standing before a man with a blade in one hand and holding a broken bottle by the neck in the other hand. Gabe deflected his cutlass but the man jabbed him in the upper arm. The sharp glass cut right through the coat's cloth and Gabe could feel glass break off in his arm.

Gabe, falling back, was able to pull a pistol and shoot the man in the face. The arm was bleeding freely but it didn't hurt too badly unless Gabe used it. Letting his sword fall, and putting the lanyard over his wrist and holding it, he pulled another pistol and shot a man in the back as he was joining his mate attacking Hex.

The next thing Gabe knew, Noble was beside him. He ran his blade through a Spaniard's neck, severing the carotid artery. Noble and Gabe were both sprayed as the man's life blood pumped out of his body. Finally, he fell into one of his mates. As the man turned, Noble lunged with his blade. The man grabbed the blade as he fell, almost pulling Noble with him. Noble had to put his foot on the man's chest and yank to retrieve his blade.

Gabe looked about him and saw that *Warlock's* men had basically overwhelmed the enemy. He was feeling weak and blinked to rid himself of the dizziness that was creeping up on him. Had the man not yelled as he attacked, Gabe would have died then and there. But the fool's victory shout cost him his life.

Gabe threw up his blade to block the Don captain's attack. It was more reflex than skill. The clang as steel banged on steel echoed across the ship. The force of the blow numbed Gabe's arm all the way to his shoulder. Spinning, more by accident to keep from falling, Gabe's blade parried the enemy just in the nick of time. The fog in Gabe's brain cleared with this jolt. The Don captain swung at Gabe's head. Had it landed, it would have cut his head off. Gabe thought, '*so the Don captain liked to sever heads*'. The man lunged half-heartedly. Gabe could have easily blocked the attack and did but only at the last second, making the captain think that he was worse off than he really was.

A smile creased the enemy captain's face. "I think, Señor that you are about done for."

"No matter," Gabe hissed. "We've taken your ship."

Anger flew over the Spaniard. With a fury, he went for Gabe's head again. Only this time, Gabe was ready. As the man raised his blade to slash, Gabe took a quick step forward and his blade glanced off his intended target, the Don's wide open chest. Instead, it bounced up and entered under the chin and came out the top of the captain's head.

One of the dead captain's crew crossed himself as he uttered, "Santa Maria."

It was over. The fighting had stopped as they all watched the commodore and Spanish captain battle it out. Gabe's blade made a sucking sound as he withdrew it from the captain's body. Gabe amazed everyone then, as he swung his blade viciously, severing the Don's head from his body.

CHAPTER THIRTY THREE

"HELP ME BACK TO the ship, Jake," Gabe said. As they turned, both Noble and Captain Skidmore were there.

"See if that ship will stay afloat until we get back to Antigua. Troy!"

"Yes, sir," Troy replied.

"Put the Dago's head in some spirits. We'll send it home," Gabe said.

"Just his head, Commodore?" Troy asked.

"Aye, just the head," Gabe replied.

With the marines at the swivels, Noble had the crew of *La Cazadora* putting the ship back together as much as possible. Just as the commodore had said, 'so she'll float.'

Warlock's bosun got his men together clearing the wreckage. *Warlock's* carpenters and mates were hard at stopping the few leaks, most of them were sprung planks below the waterline, but the beautiful *Warlock* had been damaged above the waterline, also. A big hole stood where an eighteen pound cannon had been. Spars needed to be replaced. Lanterns were lit to help the crew see to go about doing the repairs.

The glowing lanterns acted as a beacon for Midshipman Rawls and Harris, the bosun's mate. They had picked up the girls clinging to the hatch cover. After getting the girls on board the ship's boat and then lashing the hatch cover to the side, the four of them watched in awe as the flames from the ships' actions lit up the night.

"I prayed that your ship would win," one of the girls said.

"We all did," Harris replied.

"Otherwise, we'd be in a fickle," the other girl said.

"We'll win," Rawls had responded, matter-of-factly. "The commodore ain't never lost, his cox'n, Hex, told me. A damn Dago captain ain't likely to be the first."

Harris didn't reply.

***

GABE WAS TAKEN TO the captain's cabin. Felix ran for the surgeon as Hex helped Gabe out of his coat. The sleeve was sodden with blood. The girl, Roberta, came up. She brought her forceps, bandage material, and suture material. She cleaned the clotted blood away, and expertly removed the broken shards of glass. She was as gentle as she could be, but one large piece proved difficult. Roberta had decided to give up when the piece came loose. There was no way of piecing the glass together to see if she got it all, so after bathing the wound in warm water, she lightly ran her fingers over the wound, finding one more piece. After removing it and cleansing the wound, the commodore was given a warm tea with drops of laudanum in it. Once the commodore went to sleep, Roberta sewed the wound as expertly as any seamstress.

By the time she had finished, the surgeon, Pilcher, was there. He felt around checking for any glass that may have been missed. He then tugged on the sutures. "Better than I could do. Did you pour whiskey over the wound?" he asked.

"Yes, before sewing it," Roberta replied.

He looked at Hex. "It's said that helps keep the wound from suppuration," Pilcher said, by way of explanation.

"Our old surgeon, Doctor Cornish, would do that," Hex responded. "He'd pour it over his hands, at times, as well."

"Well good," Pilcher said.

When Gabe came to the following morning, it was after rolling onto his injured arm. Felix heard him cry out, and called to Jake Hex as he went to get the surgeon. Gabe was sitting up when Hex entered.

Hex smiled seeing the commodore sitting up. "How goes it today?"

Gabe replied, "I feel hung over but not bad."

"How's your arm?" Both men turned to see the surgeon and Roberta.

"Better than last night," Gabe answered, pulling the sheet up closer around his waist. He asked, "Who undressed me?"

"Several of us helped," Hex said.

Roberta smiled when the commodore flushed. "I didn't peep," she said, smiling.

The arm was red and a little tender around the wound. "You did a good job, Roberta. If the wound heals well, maybe the commodore will give you a recommendation for surgeon's mate," Pilcher said.

"She did this?" Gabe asked.

"Every bit," Hex quipped.

Gabe took a breath and gave a sigh as he worked his fingers and felt his arm where it was wounded. "Thank you," he said to the girl. "I'll give you that letter."

"You should," Hex said. "That arm was a mangled mess."

Gabe nodded, "Just let me know when." After dressing, he made it to the table where Felix gave him a cup of coffee and a tart.

Captain Skidmore came down and said, "Noble has the Don ship. He's the only lieutenant that I have left. Things are going good. *Active* was sighted with their prize. I don't see the mail packet, so maybe they sailed on to Barbados."

Gabe said, "I'll be up in a bit."

"Rest, Commodore," Troy replied. "We are doing well, right now."

***

CAPTAIN RONALD LAQUA CAME on board HMS *Warlock*. His trained eye told him quickly that the Dagos had made a fight of it. Captain Skidmore had met Laqua at the entry port. He quickly told Laqua that the commodore had been wounded but was recovering. Gabe was sitting up at the dining table when Laqua walked in.

He quickly saw the sling but also the paleness. Sir Gabe had lost blood, so much so, that his color was not good. He swallowed and spoke, "You are not trying to get on the doctor's sick, lame, and lazy list are you, sir?"

Gabe smiled, "We waited but you were too busy, it seems, so we made a go of it."

"Tis sorry I am, Sir Gabe. The damnable Don wanted to make a fight of it. It was near dark before we finally took them."

"What was the butcher's bill, Ron?" Gabe asked.

"Six dead and sixteen wounded," Laqua replied.

Gabe nodded and responded, "*Warlock* had thirteen dead and thirty wounded." A total of nineteen dead and forty-six wounded, it was a hard price to pay.

Seeing the grieved look on Gabe's face, Laqua spoke, "It was those damn big twenty-four pound cannons, sir. I only had half their weight and even *Warlock* had to get close to use her big smashers."

"Aye," Gabe said. "It did make a difference, plus Christie had his crews firing them at a far greater rate than the Dons could fire their twenty-four pounders."

Laqua stayed with Gabe through a glass of hock. "Is there anything that I can do?" he asked, speaking to both Troy and the commodore.

"If you have a senior mid to help out," Troy said. "We are without any lieutenants, other than Mr. Stanhope."

"I have one who passed the exam," Captain Laqua offered.

"Send him over," Troy said smiling.

After Captain Laqua left, Hex came in. "The Puerto Rican girls would like to speak to you, sir. Basically, they want to thank you."

"Jake, have you learned if they were molested?" Gabe inquired.

"They were by the ship's captain. The men had been promised the two girls. However, Captain Alvarado kept the girls for himself, promising to take all the women off the next ship they came on, to give to the men. Luckily, we came upon the mail packet before they could take her. I don't know if it had any women on board, but if they had..."

Gabe shook his head and thought; *at least the two girls were not given to the crew.* The captain was bad enough. The girls would likely have killed themselves had they been ravaged by the *La Cazadora* crew. "Send them down then, Jake."

Marianna and Consuelo were beautiful young ladies. Gabe was not sure if the proper term was Spanish heritage or Puerto Rican heritage, but the girls looked much more mature than English girls of the same age. They thanked Gabe for their rescue and when he implied that they had been searching for them at Pepe's request, they really seemed happy. They could not believe Pepe, fat little Pepe, would sail his little ship to the British stronghold to seek help.

Pepe was certainly elevated in their minds. Gabe invited the women to dine, thinking it would be better than the alternative. When he told them that he'd send them back to San Juan, they were all giggles. When they left the cabin, Gabe asked Felix to have Roberta attend him.

"Are you not well," Roberta asked when she entered.

Gabe smiled, "I'm healing well, thanks to you." Roberta smiled back at him.

He hesitated, took a breath and spoke, "Roberta, at your age, I'm sure you are aware of certain acts that men and women do on occasion. Like the Bible says, two become one."

"Are you asking if I am knowledgeable about sex, Sir Gabe?" she asked.

"Yes," Gabe said.

"I come from a village where boys were forever trying to get my drawers off, so yes, I'm aware of sex," she said.

"Good, I mean I see. You are aware of the two girls we rescued," he asked.

"Yes, sir," Roberta replied.

"They were ...ere used by the Spanish captain. I would be grateful if you would talk to them and see if they have any medical concerns. I would prefer that we not take them home without having provided treatment if it is needed," Gabe said.

"I will be glad to talk with them, sir," she responded.

"Thank you, Roberta. When we get to Antigua, I would like for you to talk with our surgeon on *Centaur*. He is a medical doctor and not just a surgeon," Gabe said.

"Thank you, Commodore," she replied.

As she turned to leave, another thought occurred

to Gabe. "If you would accept it, Roberta, please come and dine with my wife and I." Roberta looked down at her clothes. "Don't worry about the clothes. Knowing my wife, she'll be happy to take you shopping." He could see the girl hesitating. "Please, Roberta, Faith and I would be honored."

"Yes, sir."

CHAPTER THIRTY FOUR

GABE COULDN'T REMEMBER A time when Fort Berkeley looked so good. A big crowd had gathered on shore, seeing the return of the British ships with two prizes. It was not long before two people had made their way to HMS *Warlock*. One of them was Lord Skalla, and the other was Rear Admiral Gardner.

Gabe summarized the actions that took place and the desire to sail *La Cazadora* to San Juan to deliver the girls and the head of Capitan de Fragata Juan Alvarado. "I think that it would send a message."

"Aye," Lord Skalla agreed, "Alas, it may cost us heads of our own. Seeing that Gabe didn't like his answer, Lord Skalla spoke again. "You are a man of action, a warrior if you will. There's no doubt about Gabe Anthony. He will cross swords or pistols with anyone who threatens what's his. Unfortunately, countries are not always so open. There are as many deals made in bed chambers or out of the way pubs, as there are battles on the field or at sea. Believe me, Gabe; your deeds will not go unnoticed. Spain will openly deny any knowledge of Alvarado and Monterio. They will claim they are renegades or pirates. But we know, and the important thing is that they know we know. That is enough...it has to be enough. Even with your great contribution last year, England cannot afford another war right now."

When Skalla made his departure, Gabe turned to Rear Admiral Gardner. "I would like to make a short voyage on *La Cazadora*, sir, if she could be made seaworthy."

"Do you anticipate any action?" Gardner asked.

"I do not," Gabe replied.

Gardner smiled, "I have nothing pressing and I see no reason for her not to undergo a few sea trials to ascertain if the cost of repairing her is worth the expense."

Gabe followed his friend to *Warlock's* entry port to see him over the side. Gardner said, "There's a dispatch vessel in port. I'm sure it will wish to get underway after you have written your report to the Admiralty. I'm equally sure that Lord Skalla and Leo will take passage on it. Especially, if there was to be a volunteer to pass along any dispatches to Jamaica."

Gabe smiled, "It's no wonder that they made you admiral, sir." Gardner smiled at Gabe like the conspirator he was.

Once the admiral was gone, Gabe spoke to Hex, "Give this purse to Roberta. It has twenty pounds in it. Tell her to buy herself something nice with it."

"You mean a dress," Hex replied.

Gabe nodded and said, "In London, it would barely scratch the surface for a full ensemble as Faith would buy. It will get her out of those slops, though, and into something a bit more presentable. Oh...one more thing, Jake. Make sure my trophy is taken over to *Centaur*. Tell Joseph Morales, I want a waterproof box made that the item will fit into."

"You plan on sending it to Spain?" Hex asked.

"No, I'm sending it to Pepe. It's to let him see that we don't take it lightly when vermin mistreat our women. What he does with it after that is of no concern of mine."

"You have a mischievous side to you, Commodore. I'm not sure that certain men are fully aware to the fullest extent of it," Hex replied.

"They don't need to know," Gabe responded.

On deck, a bosun's chair had been rigged to lower Marianna and Consuelo over the side into the boat that would take them to Government House, where they would stay until they were given passage to San Juan. Seeing Gabe, they squealed in delight and ran to give him a kiss on the side of the face. The new lieutenant, Mister Gage, retrieved them and got them back to the bosun's chair.

"My apology, sir, I hope that you were not bothered," Gage said.

Gabe waved the new lieutenant away, "I'm fine, sir."

Troy Skidmore walked up to Gabe, and saw the broad pennant was still flying, and flapping in the breeze. "It's been a pleasure having you, Sir Gabe. I hope that you will give us the chance to fly your pennant again sometime."

Gabe looked at Troy and smiled, "I have something in mind, Troy. I will speak with you about it later."

***

AS ANTICIPATED, FAITH HAD gotten word that her man was back and had the carriage waiting at the waterfront. She was out of the carriage very quickly, after seeing Gabe's arm in a sling.

"You are hurt!" she exclaimed.

"It is nothing serious," he said, as he pulled her to him and kissed her.

Gabe told Faith, that night at home, about Robert, who turned out to be Roberta. He also told her of the battle, but leaving out the severity of it. He was enjoying the bath that Faith was giving him. The freshness of the water running over him felt good. Faith was in a gauzy shift that had gotten wet as she sponged water over her husband. Seeing her breasts pushed against the new see through material aroused him.

He stood and pulled her to him, "My God, woman, you know how to set a man's humors boiling."

Faith laughed and said, "Me, an old wench in the family way."

"You are a beautiful wench to me," he said. He pulled the shift off of her, stepping on it as he stepped from the tub. He felt a bit of pain and a slight pull at his wound as he lifted her and took her to the bed. "You don't know how much I've missed you since we left," Gabe whispered."

The candle beside the bed gave a faint glow to the bedroom. Faith saw an increase in the white of Gabe's hair. A widening of the gray furrow that a ball from a musket had left years ago. How many battles had her man fought? Each one seemed to weigh on him more and more. She could tell by the way he held her, clinging to her. She knew that he would be old before his time. He was now twenty-eight years old. He'd been on a ship for most of his life, and he'd faced nearly every hardship that the sea could throw at him. He'd walked the quarterdeck of his own ship most of the last ten years. She'd heard Dagan say that Gabe would give him a niece and nephews. Would he, would they? Nanny was adamant that Faith carried a son. If true, that would be two sons.

She heard a door closing downstairs; it was Jake Hex coming in. He had had a late night. He had probably visited Zelda Townsend. Faith had seen her, and she was a very beautiful and exotic woman. Did she remind Jake of the woman from Grand Cayman? Zelda was said to be a quadroon, but she had none of the black features. Here on the island, nothing would be said about the relationship, nor in England as long as she was just his mistress. But a marriage would never be accepted. Jake was not likely thinking of marriage, not this evening anyway.

***

Hex was waiting on Roberta Palmer. She went into the dress shop in seaman's slops and came out in a dress that she'd bought last week and they'd made a few alterations. The other side of the dress shop was the tailor that No had used for his new lieutenant's uniforms. He had been passing the time of day with Hex when Roberta walked out. Both of the men were astonished at how beautiful Roberta was.

She flushed, seeing the men look at her. "Is something wrong?" she asked.

"Nothing," Jake muttered. "It's just that I'm not used to seeing you this way." *Damn*, Jake thought, *if all those men in her old mess could see her now*.

No took a step forward and held out his hand. She reached out and No took it. "Let me introduce myself, Madam, I'm Lieutenant Noble Stanhope."

Roberta flushed, "I know you, sir, I was in your division."

No smiled, "You couldn't have been, I would never forget such a beautiful creature as yourself." He suddenly recalled her breasts jutting out when her top had been ripped from her body. Watching, Hex thought that she might be competition for Gretchen.

A moment later, Roberta said, "Will you be joining us tonight?"

"Wild horses couldn't keep me away, but unfortunately, a duty roster will," No replied.

Roberta knew this dashing lieutenant had a special relationship with the commodore, as did Hex. She'd seen the commodore come topside when Noble had the middle watch and spend an hour talking to the boy. Boy...he was scarcely older than her ... *if* he was older. He was a seasoned officer and he'd just made lieutenant. All the men liked him. She was suddenly very glad that he had survived the battle. She didn't think any man could make her heart beat like this young officer did. Playing the part of a male, she'd heard the crude discussions about women in the mess. She was out of that now, hopefully, she'd never go back.

The dinner that evening proved to be a grand affair. Captain Davy and his wife, Ariel, had been there, as well. Jake Hex had eaten with them and then left. While the women sat and talked, Gabe and Davy walked outside.

"Faith and Ariel have sure taken to Roberta," Davy said. He then added, "You don't intend for her to go on board a ship, do you?"

Shaking his head, Gabe said, "No." Puffing on his pipe to get it going, he said, "She has nothing and since her father died, she has no one. Doctor Honeycutt says that she is very skillful and thought she'd make a good surgeon's mate or a nurse. He will talk to the chief surgeon at the hospital tomorrow. We'll have to find her a place to live."

Laughter sounded from the house. "Gabe," Davy said. "I wonder if Ariel would like for us to take her in."

Gabe took another puff on his pipe. "I had intended to ask Faith the same thing, but Gretchen is coming back."

Davy nodded, "I'll speak to Ariel about it tonight."

EPILOGUE

"LAND HO!"

Gabe knew that would be Puerto Rico. They had taken *La Cazadora* out for the 'sea trials' as he and Admiral Gardner had discussed. They had put together a crew of volunteers to sail the ship. Lieutenant Noble Pride Stanhope had been put in command of the ship. The rest of the crew were mostly petty officers and seamen. Two master's mates were on board to share the watch. Joseph Morales had even volunteered to make the trip.

Looking toward the stern, Gabe could see HMS *Thorn*. She was a beautiful sight to Gabe. *In regards to sure beauty, it was a tossup between a ship rigged sloop of war with their flushed decks, and a frigate,* Gabe thought. While the seventy-four's up to the one-hundred gun ships of the line impressed people with their overwhelming look of power, it was the smaller ships that were beautiful.

Gabe turned to look, hearing laughter, it was Marianna and Consuelo. They were talking to Morales. Maybe that was why the carpenter had volunteered to come. Gabe thought it would have been enough for him. Morales, however, had done a good job going through the ship. Midshipman Marty Mahan from *Centaur* had followed the carpenter around taking notes.

Looking at the girls, Roberta came to Gabe's mind. She had talked to the girls and both girls had said that while they had been used by Captain Alvarado, he had not been their first sexual encounter. They had confided to Roberta that having been taken had actually turned out to be a blessing. They no longer had to worry about explaining to the priest or future husbands why they were not virgins. *Had Alvarado turned them over to the crew, they wouldn't have thought it a blessing*, Gabe thought. His other thought, in regards to Roberta, was a good one. Captain David Davy and Ariel had decided to take the girl in as their ward.

He recalled seeing the glow on her face after Faith and Ariel had taken her shopping. The dresses alone had cost Davy a few thousand pounds, and that didn't include all the trimmings. The chief surgeon at the hospital was scheduled to dine at Davy's house to discuss the training for Roberta.

Hex walked up, "They are closing with the harbor and about to begin the salute."

"Thanks for the warning," Gabe responded. If Jake had not alerted him, he would have been shocked. "Have you noticed how well No handles this ship?"

"Aye, I have."

Gabe said, "But with us being at peace, it will be a while before he walks his own quarterdeck, I'm thinking."

Hex smiled, "Not like our commodore and flag captain."

Gabe smiled at his cox'n and friend. "I don't know if it was worth it, Jake. I'm sure that Dagan would say for us, at least, the only good things to come out of the war would be Faith and Betsy. I'd add to that, though."

The big cox'n stood waiting for Gabe to finish. "What would the other thing be, sir?"

"You, Jake...you and your friendship. Your loyalty to me and my family," Gabe replied.

"Thank you, sir. I feel honored to hear you say that," Jake responded.

***

GABE HAD RETURNED THE girls to Pepe and his wife, and it was a joyous reunion. He asked Pepe to visit him on board the *La Cazadora* after he'd made his official visits.

The mayor and Captaincy General welcomed Gabe as a distinguished guest. He alluded that the reason for his visit was to return Marianna and Consuelo to their parents. Gabe went on to say that two pirate ships had been raiding shipping lines from Bermuda to Venezuela. He was sure the kidnapping of the girls had been reported. However, the pirates would bother no more ships or people in San Juan, as the ships in his squadron had hunted them down and ended their reign of piracy.

The men, who had looked a bit worried when Gabe had arrived, were openly smiling now. They had seen the British commodore arrive in *La Cazadora,* now named the *Huntress*. The ship was like no other in the Caribbean, so it had been recognized immediately. With the British flag flying from her staff, the men could only guess at the repercussions that might come their way. Both men were obviously relieved, so they wanted to have the commodore and his officers dine with them that evening. Gabe politely declined, citing duty, but invited the men to visit Antigua. Since the commodore couldn't stay, they treated him to two boxes of Cuban cigars and a case of Sangria wine.

Gabe was taken back to the ship, after the meeting, via the captaincy general's official carriage. Within an hour, little Pepe came on board as Gabe had asked him to do. On the captain's desk sat a box with a little lock on it. Pepe saw it immediately upon being ushered into the commodore's cabin.

"Are you squeamish?" Gabe asked. When the man didn't understand the question, Josh spoke to Pepe in Spanish.

"No, Commodore," Pepe replied.

Gabe pointed to the nicely made wooden box. "It's yours," he said.

Pepe opened the box and lifted the large jar out of it. "Santa Maria," he said, as he almost dropped the jar, and then clutched it to him tightly.

"That is all that remains of the man who kidnapped and abused your girls," Gabe said. "I thought that you'd like to see how I treat murderers and rapists, Pepe. If you don't want the gift, I will toss it overboard when we clear the harbor."

"Oh no, Señor! I will place it in a very prominent place to be seen by all. It will let villains and rapists know better than to mess with Pepe's family. It will also speak of the friendship we share," Pepe replied.

"Aye," Gabe responded and shook Pepe's hand.

Within an hour of weighing anchor and leaving San Juan, the word had spread until it reached the mayor, and then the captaincy general. They went to see this example of what Pepe's friends would do to someone who murdered and abused women. The mayor and captaincy general saw it as an omen beyond what happened to folks who bothered Pepe's family. It said, to them, this was the penalty to be expected if you harmed British citizens. The commodore had gotten his point across in a vivid manner.

***

THE CARRIAGE WAS WAITING at the waterfront when they returned to English Harbor. A mail packet was spotted as they anchored. Hex had seen the family carriage and had quickly found Gabe and whispered to him.

Gabe walked over to No. "Captain," he said, with a

smile, "you'll need to report to Admiral Gardner that you have returned his ship. You may as well go on shore with me."

"Aye, Sir Gabe," No responded.

The ship's boat ground into the sandy beach and a seaman jumped out and pulled it further up on the beach. Gabe and Noble walked to the carriage.

Noble saw Faith jump out...no, Faith didn't jump out, it was Gretchen. It was such a passionate embrace and kiss, Gabe turned his head as No crushed Gretchen to him. Hex was smiling at the couple.

"You're back," No finally said.

"Yes, darling, if you'll have me, I'm back, back for eternity," Gretchen replied.

Faith and Gabe hugged and kissed. "It's over?" Faith asked.

Gabe smiled and nodded, "It's over, dear. We are finally at peace." It was a peace that was a long time in coming.

Faith hugged him again, feeling her baby bump press against her husband. "It will be a new beginning for us," she said. "It is one that I've longed for."

Seeing No and Gretchen still entwined, Gabe said, "Another new beginning it appears."

Faith turned to see the two lovers. Sounding as much like a sailor as she could, Faith said, "Aye."

Three months later on November 19, 1794, a son was born, Jacob Gabriel Anthony.

IT WAS A TIME FOR PEACE!!!

Author's note: This the last book in the Fighting Anthonys series. I want to thank all the loyal readers who made it possible to keep this series going for ten books. While I end this series at the end of the American Revolutionary War, I intend to try my hand at England's war with France. Many of these same characters will be included in that series. Several of the characters are also included in my trilogy, *The Pyrate.*

About the Author

Michael Aye is a retired Naval Medical Officer. He has long been a student of early American and British Naval history. Since reading his first Kent novel, Mike has spent many hours reading the great authors of sea fiction, often while being "haze gray and underway" himself.

www.ingramcontent.com/pod-product-compliance
Lightning Source LLC
La Vergne TN
LVHW050622100826
845148LV00011B/1695

* 9 7 8 1 6 8 5 5 3 0 3 3 4 *